What people are saying about Jenny Gardiner's books:

Red Hot Romeo
"Awesome". So enjoyed the romantic chemistry between the two characters. Read it non stop into the wee hours. Highly recommend this book
-- Mrs. K

Blue-Blooded Romeo
"Another brilliant, fun read from Jenny Gardiner. The book is fun to read and I thoroughly enjoyed every word. Jenny Gardiner has put the fun back into romance books and I look forward to each book in this delightful series."
-- Anne Blyth

"I had planned on only reading a few chapters at first but couldn't put it down. A terrific storyline, well-developed and extremely relatable characters, what's not to love?? Great read!"
-- Samantha Reeves

Big O Romeo
"I could not put this book down. Warning don't start this book late at night as you will not want to stop reading.
-- Di

Sleeping with Ward Cleaver

"A fun, sassy read! A cross between Erma Bombeck and Candace Bushnell, reading Jenny Gardiner is like sinking your teeth into a chocolate cupcake...you just want more."

--Meg Cabot, NY Times bestselling author of Princess Diaries, Queen of Babble and more

Slim to None

"Jenny Gardiner has done it again--this fun, fast-paced book is a great summer read."

--Sarah Pekkanen, NY Times bestselling author of *The Opposite of Me*

Hard to Get Over

(Book Three of the Hard to Get Series)

by Jenny Gardiner

http://jennygardiner.net/

Chapter One

THERE'S no such thing as a good funeral, but if there were, Daphne Sweeney would give herself a tiny pat on the back for having executed it. After spending years as a daily lifeline to her elderly neighbor Violet Nicholson, it fell to Daphne to organize the final memorial for Violet, who apparently left behind no living relatives and a smattering of friends. Violet had passed in her sleep at the age of ninety-two, and Daphne took no pleasure in being the one to find her that morning. Still, she was relieved that Violet likely hadn't suffered. It was her first encounter with a dead person and a little unsettling for sure. But she immediately took control of the situation, had the appropriate authorities declare Violet officially expired, and planned the service, which was only attended by a few neighbors who knew her from when she'd sit on the porch stoop and wave to passersby, before she got too old and weak and the task became too onerous.

It was a sobering lesson for Daphne, who'd become a bit too much of a homebody over the past couple of years, working at home as a graphic designer since all of her customers were online. Not having to go to an office sounded perfect, but in reality, she'd lost touch with too many people. Instead of taking time off at the end of the workday, she discovered herself working more waking hours than she should. Her personal life—which, let's be honest, was nonexistent anyhow—and her work life had blurred into one. Seeing how Violet died alone was eye-opening: did Daphne want to stumble along into old age, becoming a shut-in, friendless and loveless, void of any romantic relationship, married to her job rather than a man who cared about her? Violet had never been married and had relied on her sister for companionship until she'd passed away a decade earlier. Was that what Daphne had to look forward to—a gaping maw of loneliness?

Not that Violet had always been lonely—Daphne knew that before she'd become too infirm, Violet had played canasta with a local group on a regular basis. She took daily walks through the neighborhood, waving at all the neighbors. Sometimes she'd hire a taxi to attend concerts at the Kennedy Center or visit the Smithsonian's National Portrait Gallery when she really got wild.

Over the years, Daphne grew to love Violet like the mother she'd lost as a teenager. And she cared for her as she would have her own. She brought meals to her most days and sat with her over coffee as they lamented the state of the world today, and Violet reassured her that things were always bad on some level and not to fret about it too much. They'd watch movies or Netflix or play Scrabble, which Violet always won, and it would be almost like a date, minus the making out and heavy petting. *Heavy petting.* Daphne rolled her eyes. She'd forgotten what that even was. Except when it came to her white Labrador, Tortellini, who was the love of her life and deserved lots of petting. She'd heavy-pet Tortellini to the moon and back.

Heaving a heavy sigh, Daphne resolved to do something about the fact that she did nothing and her life was an empty void.

Well, maybe tomorrow.

It wasn't a but a week or so after the memorial service that Daphne got the letter in the mail.

> My dearest Daphne,
>
> I hope you realize that you have been like a daughter to me for many years, and I have been forever grateful for your willingness to amuse this old gal and treat me like family. For all intents and purposes, you have been my only family, but for a second nephew twice removed or some such nonsense. I never could get those things right. Maybe he's a grandnephew? One of those things. I was prepared to leave quite literally everything to you, however I made a promise long ago to my sister that I would include him as a beneficiary of my estate upon my death. She said he's a wanderer and she worried he was too broke to settle down.
>
> My largest asset is this duplex that you've been renting from me for the past however many years. I know you've worked hard to sock away money to eventually buy a place, but I'd like you to

stop worrying about that. So, I am leaving the entire contents of my life to you, and the actual home to both you and my grandnephew, or whatever he is to me. I've hardly seen him for years, so I'm sure he will be happy to do whatever you'd like as far as the property is concerned. I'm only including him to appease my beloved sister. Plus, I've heard he's grown into a handsome young man. You know you could use a handsome young man in your life.

Daphne laughed. It was so like Violet to try to matchmake even beyond the grave. Try as she might over the years, never once did any of her many fix-ups stick. Always some friend's grandson or nephew, or so-and-so said someone at canasta knew a handsome young man and did anyone know of a girl who might want to date him? Daphne humored Violet by going along on the mostly awful set-up dates. Gave her a chance to try a new drink at a bar or a restaurant she'd been meaning to check out. But usually, the guys were duds. As this one would be, no doubt.

I have left instructions with my attorney to reach out to you both. He'll help you do what's needed so you no longer have to rent and can finally become a homeowner. Always remember, I love you, Daphne. You're the daughter I never had.
Much love,
Violet

Daphne gasped. Violet had left the bulk of the estate to her? That was far too generous. How could she accept it? But with Violet gone, how could she not? She looked around her place. All these years it felt like a place where she was parking her things, not a home in which to grow roots. But now she could own it outright, and it would be her real forever home. She couldn't believe her good fortune. It was starting to look like tomorrow was finally here: she could get her act together and start living her best life.

Chapter Two

BRADY McGovern was giving some real thought to settling down. Sometime soon. And why not now? He'd been wandering for a long time. Traveling, picking up odd jobs, traveling some more. Returning home to Seattle every now and then to see some friends, but never feeling a strong enough pull to stay there. With his parents gone and no siblings, it wasn't quite the same.

Frankly, the itinerant life wasn't abnormal to Brady. Having grown up in a military family, he never did feel particularly planted anywhere. With one year here, two years there, he got to enjoy living abroad, which was cool, but he also never experienced continuity, which was tough as a kid. The longest time he stayed in one place was during college in North Carolina. Four years in Chapel Hill was great but more than enough time in one town.

He'd taken off the day after graduation. His only regret was flaking out on a girl he'd recently started dating. Never even told her goodbye, just left. He figured it was easier that way. It wasn't like they'd been serious or anything, anyhow. He needed the freedom of the open road, no ties holding him back. At first, he wandered around the States, camping and hiking in national parks. He even set about to hike the tallest mountain in each state. It took him two years, but he did it.

Just in time to learn that his parents had died in a small plane crash. He'd never had a chance to say goodbye.

That hit him hard. Afterward he took off for parts unknown. Bought a plane ticket to India and went from there to a number of continents over the next several years. Sure, insurance money from his folks' estate gave him the luxury of wandering aimlessly. And for a while it helped him to seek out the rest of the world, to try to make sense of it all having gone sideways for him.

He was in line waiting to board a flight to London when he glanced down at his phone and noticed an email from some law firm, which was weird, because it wasn't like he dealt with attorneys for anything.

He opened the email and scanned it quickly before boarding the plane, where he'd lose the Wi-Fi. His eyes scanned the words. Great-Aunt Violet. Property in Washington, DC area. She was leaving it to him and some woman who rented half of the place from her to divvy up however they saw fit. Huh. Weird. He vaguely remembered meeting her. Was she like his mother's aunt's sister or something like that? Hell, he had no idea. Growing up, he and his folks were never around enough to spend time with family.

The gate person announced the final boarding call and Brady stuck his phone in his pocket. He'd deal with that later.

Two weeks later, it was wheels down at Washington Dulles airport. He intended to check out this windfall he hadn't expected. The attorney had sent him the key and the address and he was now in an Uber on his way to the house. He figured he'd spend a couple of days meeting with folks about unloading the place—properties in the DC area were selling like gangbusters—and get on the road as soon as it was all under control.

By the time he arrived at the house, the sky was darkening. A light drizzle came down as he exited the Uber. Approaching the house, he stumbled on some broken piece of concrete on the walkway. He squinted and gave the place a long look. Huh. It was like two identical houses in one. One side was pitch black; the other had lights on. He turned on the light on his phone to avoid any more tripping hazards and arrived at the door, dropping his heavy backpack on the ground with a thud. Grabbing the key from his pocket, he fumbled around to fit it into the deadbolt keyhole.

When at last he got the key in and turned the lock, the porch light of the adjacent home came on and a dog barked.

"Who are *you?*" came a stern, accusatory female voice behind him.

He jiggled the key out as he opened the door.

"Oh hey, I'm Violet's, well, Violet was my, well, some sort of aunt," he said, turning around and reaching out his hand. "Brady. Brady McGovern. And you are?"

The woman did a double-take and then for a long, awkward beat stared at him, wide-eyed, decidedly not extending her hand. The cute dog happily licked it, however, until she pulled the animal away.

"Brady *McGovern?*" She squinted, then snarled her lip. If she were an apex predator, he'd be worried she was going to pounce. And not in a good way. "As in Brady-the-dirty-ratfink-who-evaporated-into-thin-air-the-day-after-graduation-McGovern?"

He lifted a brow. Huh. That didn't sound so good. He pushed his sunglasses up onto his head, not even noticing until then that he'd still had them on. No wonder it was so damned dark. And then he finally saw who was standing in front of him.

"Uh, Daphne?" He frowned. Daphne was her name, wasn't it? Right—Daphne Sweeney. What were the chances the woman he'd dumped when he left to check out of the real world would be the person he apparently had to sell this place with? Smiling, he went in for a hug, arms outstretched. "Hey! Daphne! Great to see you!"

She stood stock-still, her arms tightly pressed to her sides. Clearly no hug was imminent.

"*Great to see you?* Are you freaking kidding me? I can't think of anyone I'd rather not see at this very minute. Or any other time, for that matter."

The cute dog came and jumped up against his chest, licking his face. At least somebody was glad to see him. He'd take advantage of a warm reception from any creature with a pulse and scratched the dog's head and ears.

"Look, Daph—"

"Don't 'Daph' me."

"I'm sorry, Daphne." He scrubbed his hands over his face. "It's late. I'm tired. I'm on Greenwich Mean Time or something like that. Looks like we've got some figuring out to do. What say we meet over coffee in the morning to come up with a game plan?"

She glared at him. "Yeah, right. Last time I had plans to meet with you the next day, I never saw you again."

He shook his head. Damn, even angry, she was a sight for sore eyes. From where he stood, she looked even hotter than she did in college. Tall, with an athletic build, gorgeous set of tits, and a tight little butt, she was stunning even in shorts and a thin tee. Despite being filled with fury at the moment, her blue eyes were still mesmerizing, kind of sexier when pissed off. And that curly, long black hair of hers—he remembered how it felt as his fingers twined through her hair when she went down on him. Well, shit. Maybe that was the wrong thought because now his cock swelled in his pants. Not quite the greeting she was looking for, no doubt. Hmmm… in hindsight, maybe having ditched her like that was a mistake.

"Can we talk about this later? I'm beat and need some shut-eye. We can figure out selling this thing in the morning. I'm thinking we can have it on the market in a couple of days. I did a little research. The market's superhot here right now. We'll be good to go and then I can get out of your hair." Even though the idea of tangling his fingers in that hair again sure sounded like a great diversion.

She crossed her arms across her chest. Her shapely chest that he was struggling not to stare at. "Excuse me? On the market?"

"Well, yeah. We have to sell this thing. No point in keeping it."

She gave him one of those "are you a fucking idiot?" looks, her eyes squinted, her brow knit tight. "I beg to differ. This is my home, little runaway. You might not understand the value of home, but I certainly do, and this is where I am planting my roots."

Brady scratched at the two-day-old scruff on his face. He needed a bite to eat, a stiff drink, and a bed. The last thing he needed was some pissed-off ex flipping her shit on him right now.

"Okay, well. Huh. Yeah. Um. So. Well. I'm gonna go to bed now and we'll talk tomorrow." He grabbed his backpack and pushed it into the foyer. "Good night, Daph."

As he turned to go inside, he saw her stick her middle finger right up in his line of vision.

Well, crap. This wasn't going to be the cakewalk he'd presumed after all.

Chapter Three

"GET over here, Tortellini, you Benedict Arnold." Daphne tugged on the dog's hot pink martini glass collar she so loved, pulling her pup back inside and away from the bad, bad man. She always made sure the dog was wearing that collar when she poured herself a happy hour cocktail. After all, it was better not to drink alone, and that way her dog had a glass too. How's that—her own dog betraying her by welcoming that awful man? She could hardly believe her disloyal dog dared even lick the hand of that rat bastard. Frankly she should've bitten it in defense of her owner.

We'll talk tomorrow. He had some nerve. *Talk tomorrow.* As if he didn't blow out of town like an Alberta clipper that dumped a pile of snow and was gone in an hour. Only at least those weather systems left behind something useful, so maybe you could make a snowman or go sledding. Whereas all he left behind was an embittered young woman who'd felt used and discarded and never understood what she'd done to deserve it. How on earth could that man be related to sweet, lovable Violet? It seemed impossible. And what did this mean? Would she have to deal with this traitorous jerk now? What if they had conflicting ideas about the property? He'd said something about the market being hot and selling it. But he'd better get used to the idea that she was keeping it. End of story. Violet's letter said whoever this nephew guy was would do whatever she wanted. She hadn't considered that the biggest asshole around would show up on her doorstep wanting to unload the place. Her home. *Her home.* She could not let Brady McGovern get the upper hand and sell the place out from under her, leaving her homeless. In a hot market, she'd not even be able to buy something else with whatever proceeds she ended up with. And then where would she be?

Daphne decided she needed a soothing cup of tea and then she'd do ten minutes of meditation before falling asleep for the night. It was her only hope of actually not waking in a fit of rage every hour on the hour.

It seemed like she'd barely drifted off to sleep when she heard a loud pounding on her door. She pulled her eye mask onto her forehead and saw faint traces of light seeping through the edges of the curtains, so it must've been morning, right? She glanced at her phone and saw that it was 5:55. a.m. Who pounds on someone's door at that hour, unless there's a fire and they need to get you out?

She creaked out of bed, and Tortellini, excited that the day was about to begin—like it or not—ran circles around Daphne as she walked along the short hallway and down the steps to answer the front door. She flicked on the light and peered out the security peephole only to see the face of Satan. In the form of that dirty rotten scoundrel Brady McGovern. Keeping the chain latched, she opened the door an inch or so.

"What are you doing? Why are you bothering me at this ungodly hour?"

Hard to Get Over

"Good morning, sunshine!" Brady said with an exaggerated grin. Ugh, he did always have a gorgeous smile: nice straight, white teeth and cute little dimples perfectly punctuating his mouth. One of those smiles that finds you in a mad make-out session in the middle of a fraternity party and then the next thing you know you're having wild monkey sex in the guy's room. Thank goodness she hadn't done that with him, but she might as well have under the right circumstances. "I brought you a coffee." He tried to insert it through the inhospitable crack she'd left exposed.

Daphne could barely keep her eyes open, and what minimal daylight there was pierced her retinas in a particularly rude manner. This was no way to start what was promising to be a not-so-banner day.

"How do you know I even drink coffee?" Tortellini was goosing Daphne with her wet nose, in her own way announcing she needed to go outside. The last thing Daphne wanted to do was give this man a chance to inch any closer. But it wasn't fair to Tortellini to make her wait there with legs crossed.

"Oh, fine," she said, unlatching the chain. Maybe her dog would tackle the jerk and he'd spill hot coffee on himself. But then again, maybe he'd spill it on her dog and she didn't want that. She shook her head and rolled her eyes.

Tortellini tore out of the foyer, blew past Brady, circling around briefly to give him a few nudges with her nose, and ran to the front yard where she quickly took care of business. In the meantime, Brady had insinuated his way into Daphne's home, shoving a coffee cup in one of her hands and a big box of trash bags in the other.

Daphne shook her head and wrinkled her brow. "What is this for?"

He aimed his thumb over his shoulder, toward the adjacent side of the building. "We've got a lot of cleanup to do. Turns out old Aunt Violet was a bit of a hoarder. Place is filled to the brim with shit."

Daphne gasped. "*Shit*! How dare you!" Her tired eyes grew wide with outrage. "Violet had a lovely collection of things that made her heart happy. And besides, what is it to you what's in that house? It all belongs to me!"

"To you?"

"Yes, Violet left it for me. She knew I would treat it with tender loving care."

"Care? It's a bunch of garbage that needs to be carted off to the dump." He took a swig of coffee. "Sorry, my time's all off. Been up since four. I went online and found several reputable businesses that will haul off junk within days."

"Haul off junk?" Glaring at him, she shook her head. "There will be no hauling off of anything!"

"I took the liberty of filling up a couple of trash bags already." He pointed toward three large garbage bags filled to the brim along the curb.

Her eyes grew wide. "You *what*?"

He pointed at her eye mask, still perched on her forehead. "Nice look, by the way."

She shrieked and began to pace. "Who the hell gave you permission to saunter in here and act like you own the place?"

He shrugged. "Well, I do own the place."

She pulled off her eye mask and tossed it on the nearby sofa. "*Half* the place. Apparently." Under her breath she muttered, "Curse Violet for remembering his wretched existence."

"I heard that."

Daphne lifted a brow and shrugged. "Good. In the meantime, let me make myself abundantly clear: you do not

15

have my permission to throw those things out." She pointed with unmistakable emphasis at the menacing bags. "You need to drag those back into the house this instant. And make sure you don't break anything."

"But we need to clean this place out. I want to get it listed and sold, so I can go back on the road again."

She laughed a short, unhappy laugh. "So like you to screw me and run."

He turned his head and squinted. "Come again?"

"Huh." She pursed her lips. "Probably the last words I heard out of your mouth before you left me."

He gulped. She seethed. It was all coming back to her. He'd stayed overnight at her place after graduation. Sometime before dawn, he'd taken her on the kitchen table, and then in the shower stall. They'd fallen back asleep, and later he woke her as he'd inched down her body, burying his mouth in her pussy and bringing her to climax twice. He'd joked to her about making her come again as she'd drifted back to sleep. Yet he was gone when she woke the next time. From lover to ghost in the blink of an eye.

"Look, Daphne, let's let that be water under the bridge." He ran his fingers through his wavy brown hair.

Under the bridge my ass. Why do they always want to let bygones be bygones when they're the offenders? God, she hated that he looked so good. And that he looked so much like he did the last time she saw him in the early morning light, his blue eyes twinkling. Only he was more of a man now, filled out, his shoulders and chest strong and his waist tapered in that sexy way she couldn't resist. How was it possible that this jerk had, out of the blue, just shat himself into her life like this? It had taken her too long to get over him because of the way he'd abandoned her. It left her so unable to trust a guy. Because, well, who does that? Who leaves without a word, a note, nothing? It would have been downright gentlemanly of him to dump her via text.

Closing her eyes for a minute, she put herself back to that night. They'd made love. Wait, yuck, that sounded soooo stupid and gullible when she thought of it like that, particularly knowing now that they were simply two horny college kids in the throes of a last hurrah before the real world encroached. "Made love" sounded like they cared, and while she thought they both did, clearly he hadn't, so in hindsight, she had to think of the whole affair more transactionally. They fucked.

Yet she knew that to her it was more than that. They had only been dating a couple of months, but still, it felt like they'd been together much longer. Which was all the more reason his abrupt departure stung as much as it did. It was as if they'd been teammates, but she thought they were playing to win while he was merely playing to get traded to a better team. Or something like that.

"If by 'that' you mean you ghosting me after banging me senseless for the better part of graduation night into the following morning, well then, no. I'm not going to view that as 'water under the bridge.'" She made air quotes as she used a mocking tone. "Maybe it's cool for you to just fuck and run, but it's pretty disgusting behavior, and in my book anyone who does that deserves to have a place in the Dickhead Hall of Fame."

He scrunched his nose. "There's no such thing."

She shook her head like she was talking to a complete idiot. "Well, there should be. And if there was, you'd be front and center. Your picture would be featured at the box office. On the tickets, for that matter. And there would be a giant statue of you smack-dab in the middle of it. Where you would be memorialized as the asshole that you are."

17

Hard to Get Over

He whistled long and low. "Hell hath no fury like a woman scorned."

"A woman scorned? Are you kidding me? I fell asleep thinking I was falling in love with you and woke up to realize that instead I should have always hated you. And now here you are, trying to railroad my dear friend Violet's home into a sale so you can get on the road again? And while you're at it, screw me yet again by leaving me homeless? What, is there some woman you need to sleep and run with?"

"This is not the time or place for this discussion," he said, a hint of pleading to his voice. Shame that groveling wasn't going to work for him. The day Brady ditched her was the day Daphne became Hard-hearted Hannah toward him. She had no intention of extending him even the slightest of courtesies: not for his jet lag, not for the loss of his aunt (and obviously he didn't care about that), not for his need to get back to wherever he wanted to go. But right now, she wanted to get back to sleep.

"You're right, Brady. This is not the time or place. Right now, the only thing this is the time for is me returning to sleep. So forgive me, but I've had enough of this discussion." She grabbed her eye mask and pulled it over her eyes, then slammed the door, only then realizing no way would she be able to find her way back to bed blindfolded, so she pulled it back over her head and stormed upstairs, hating the sway that Brady McGovern had on her, even all these years later.

Chapter Four

WELL, that didn't go so well. Understatement du jour. Brady shook his head and chuckled to himself as he stood on the stoop, wondering what force of nature had just plowed into him. That was one seriously ticked-off woman and he'd have to figure out a Plan B for this one.

Meanwhile, how had he never before realized what a turn-on a pissed-off woman was? 'Cause damn, her standing there all enraged at him in her flimsy little nightgown (which was not nearly as opaque as she might have believed but he'd never point it out) had gotten him all sorts of hot and bothered. Especially at the ass crack of dawn with the first glimmer of sunlight illuminating those stiff nipples. Yeah, her words greeted him one way, but those nips welcomed him the way a man wanted to be greeted in the morning. Hello, sailor. Maybe that was why he couldn't seem to focus on whatever it was she was ranting about. He could only think about how much he'd like to get his lips fastened to those things. Then maybe she'd stop the tirade and go with the flow. Surely a little male-induced pleasure would overcome her ire.

Although he could hardly blame her for thinking he was a dick. He had been a dick. A calculated one at that, if he were honest with himself. Had he been thinking about her, he'd never have bailed the way he did. But he was a dumb college guy and he wanted put his feet on the pavement and go, wherever, whenever, however. If he seriously thought about it, maybe he'd admit that he'd gotten spooked by whatever was going on between them. They had clicked so easily. The short time they'd dated seemed a lifetime, in a good way. But that had scared him—the last thing he wanted straight out of college was a relationship to anchor him.

For too long he'd been chomping at the bit to go, and he hadn't figured out how to enunciate that to her while they were dating. He'd mentioned his plans a few times, and she dismissed them. She was so convinced he'd stop with those fantasies about wandering and find a "real job." But the last thing he, of all people, wanted was to be tethered to a desk somewhere. He didn't know how to stay put, and he wasn't going to have some woman change that, even if he did have feelings for her. He figured she'd catch on at some point but she didn't. She'd even made some peripheral references to "love" and that made him even more squeamish. Love? *Hell no.* He was most definitely not getting roped into changing his dreams because she had the erroneous belief they were in love. They'd been in lust, in the best of ways. And they'd had lots of fun together, but love? That would have suggested he was willing to settle down for a woman, and that would have been impossible.

In fact, Brady truly had no appreciation for the power of romantic love and a life partnership until he lost his parents and realized how much their relationship rooted him, despite himself. They'd packed up and moved so regularly that Brady never did learn how to attach himself to anyone for long. Yet he realized too late what his mother had sacrificed to let his father have a career that required them to pick up and go at a moment's notice. The experience had given him an appreciation for love and sacrifice that he'd never quite paid attention to or appreciated when they were alive.

But a whole lot of good that was going to do him now. He needed to come to a meeting of the minds with this chick, and fast. The last thing he wanted was to have to stick around now. Clearly she wasn't the forgiving kind, and shacking up side by side with Daphne Sweeney would be a serious slice of hell.

Taking a page from Daphne's plan, Brady headed back to sleep. If you can't beat 'em, join 'em. He'd intentionally chosen to sleep on the sofa rather than in what he had pegged as the master bedroom in case his aunt—or whatever she was to him—had keeled over there. Bad juju to sleep in a death bed like that.

But that meant lying on an overly soft piece of furniture that was probably built during the Eisenhower administration and trying hard to ignore the tick-tick-tick of the grandfather clock. Not to mention the damned hourly announcements the thing made. Whoever thought a grandfather clock was a good idea? Ridiculous. Sleep would forever be elusive with that thing spouting off. He was sorely tempted to disassemble the damned clock so it would shut up, but God forbid he do that and Cranky McCrankypants next door got wind of it. She'd lop off his balls.

Finally, he couldn't take it anymore and started rifling through some chest of drawers in the dining room until he found a cache of tablecloths. He grabbed about ten of them and started tossing them atop the clock, one after the other, in the hopes of at least muffling the noise. There was a special place in hell for the dude who invented those damned clocks.

Hard to Get Over

He bet the inventor's grandfather never spoke to him again. Standing in the living room, he admired his handiwork: the thing looked like a ghost looming in the corner. Brady hoped that at least the ghost would be a little more subdued.

Brady finally woke around four, his stomach growling. If he didn't figure out a car sitch ASAP, or he'd end up gnawing on his hand. In the meantime, he went online to find something Uber Eats would deliver. He'd take a chance and order something for the surly one next door, hoping that food would be the way to her heart. More like to her soul, 'cause it wasn't like her heart was his problem. What would an irritable woman like her want for dinner, though? He didn't want to risk making her angry that he got something she hated. But he didn't dare ask in advance, for fear she'd shut him down. He wanted to try to bond over shared plates. History was rife with situations where food had helped to settle differences, wasn't it? He didn't want to go with something as mundane as pizza, which felt a little cheap. Chinese delivery seemed cliché. He decided to flip the carryout idea on its head and order Afghani food. If she'd ever eaten it, no doubt she loved it. And if she hadn't, well, it was high time she gave it a try.

Chapter Five

"YOU'RE sure you don't mind staying in tonight and watching Netflix?" Daphne said to her friend Binti Swapna who'd shown up with two bottles of wine after Daphne tried to bail on their plans to go out to a bar.

"Dude, I'm just happy I didn't have to put on makeup. Besides, you've got the most comfortable couch of anyone I know. Staying in will be totally perfect!" Binti set the bottles on the kitchen counter and rifled through the drawer to get the opener while Daphne grabbed two stemless glasses from the cabinet next to the dishwasher. Her friend cut the foil and extracted the cork from the first bottle, pouring them each a glass.

"You hungry now, or do you want to wait before we order dinner?"

"I had a late lunch, so I'm good holding off, if you are."

"K, let me scoop Tortellini's dinner into her bowl and get her fed and we can start the show."

Tortellini had been drooling nearby, already awaiting dinner, so as soon as she heard the scoop in the kibble, she was on Daphne's heels, nudging her ankles to hurry up and feed her. Daphne placed the bowl on the floor and the dog attacked it as if she hadn't eaten in a month.

"Imagine if we went at it with a meal like that," Binti said, laughing. "Like the waiter serves your food and you inhale it, using your hands and mouth."

"Right? How hilarious would it be to devour food so fast you didn't even chew it? People would be so mortified."

"I like food too much to not savor it."

"Yeah, true dat."

They plopped down on either end of the large sectional sofa, the dog in between them, and started the movie. Not ten minutes later, the doorbell rang. Tortellini jumped up from the sofa and careened to the foyer.

"Honestly, my doorbell has rung more times in the past day than in the past decade. Who is bothering me this time?" Daphne got up, padded to the door, and peered through the peephole.

"Oh, for fuck's sake. *You* again?"

"Who?" Her friend stood and walked toward the door.

"Oh my God, I haven't filled you in yet. It's this horror of a guy I had the grave misfortune of dating in college till he ghosted me the day after graduation. And the worst coincidence ever—you know how I told you that Violet left the house to me and some random distant relative?"

Binti tucked her straight black hair behind her ears and nodded.

"Well, it turns out it's the same dude. He showed up last night and is making my life a living hell."

Binti's eyes opened wide. "You want me to help you get rid of him? Should we call the police or something?"

Daphne waved her hand. "Thanks, but it's not that kind of thing. He's insinuating himself into this house situation and I'm worried he's going to cause me problems because I want to live here outright. For good." The doorbell rang again and Tortellini jumped against the door, barking. Daphne pretended to pull out her hair in exasperation. She opened the door to see his hands weighed down with paper bags. "Can I help you?" She tried hard to sound as if she was only saying it to be polite. Probably because she *was* just saying it to be polite.

He held up his bags. "I brought dinner!"

Daphne grimaced as he helped himself into the foyer. "Make yourself right at home," she growled—yes, actually growled. This guy was turning her into someone she was not.

He looked up to see Binti, arms crossed, taking in the scene, and he reached out his hand. "Hey there! I'm Brady. Hope I wasn't disrupting anything?"

Binti held up her hands. "All good." She pointed at the bags. "What'd you bring? Smells amazing."

"I ordered Afghani food. Figured it was a little more interesting than a pepperoni pizza."

"Oh, yum, I *love* Afghani food." Binti grabbed a bag, carried it to the kitchen, and set it down on the black granite counter.

Daphne leaned over and whispered into her ear, "Whose side are you on here? Let's practice a little ambivalence, here, okay?"

Binti shrugged. "Sorry, he picked my favorite food. It's not like I can say no. You understand."

Jesus. First the dog sells out, then her best friend?

Binti and Brady unloaded the packages and spread them out on the island.

"You got the soup? I *love* this soup!"

"Right? The aush soup is amazing."

Daphne rolled her eyes yet again, determined to hate this food.

"Ahhh, and the sambosay goshti. I tried to make these at home one time—it was a disaster!"

25

"You cook?" Brady rubbed his palms together after setting down the last container, like he was ready to dig in.

"I love to cook, and I bake a ton," Binti said.

Normally Daphne would pipe in and brag on her friend's dope culinary skills, but she had no intention of inserting herself into this conversation with Mr. Yuck.

"I think I'd enjoy cooking, but I've not been anywhere long enough to have a place to do it," he said. "Hostels don't do the trick, although you can bake the occasional brownie there."

"Get out—you can bake in a hostel?"

What was with the cheery chitchat? This night was rapidly going off the rails.

"Who doesn't have a place to call home at your age? Hostel kitchens? Sounds awfully lonely to me." Daphne maybe felt a little smug saying that but seriously, what the hell? He was too old to wander aimlessly, wasn't he?

"Oh, I don't know, Daph," Binti said. "I kind of admire someone who follows their heart. Is that what you do?" She pointed at Brady.

He thrust his lower lip out as he shrugged. "I guess I never gave it much consideration. I kind of go with the flow. But I suppose you could call that following your heart."

"Who 'goes with the flow' when you've been out of college for nearly a decade?" Daphne made facetious air quotes to drive home her point.

"Someone who can?" Binti held her hands up in her own sort of shrug.

Daphne turned her back to Brady and hissed at Binti, "Whose friend are you? He's the bad guy here, B. Back me up!"

"Daph, I don't even know what this is all about, but he seems nice. Plus he brought yummy food. Let's give him a chance and see what he has to say." She refilled her wine and held up the bottle. "Would you like a glass of pinot?" She nodded at Brady.

She's giving him our fucking wine? What was next? Inviting him to watch the movie with them? Or going on vacation together? *Or stealing my home right out from under me?*

Daphne closed her eyes. *Breathe, Daphne. Imagine yourself in a lush garden. Butterflies flitting about. Or better yet, make that the ocean. A gentle breeze wafts across you as you're enveloped in warm, soothing waters while you listen to the soothing sound of waves rolling onto shore. But suddenly you see a fin surfacing and you immediately scream for help, kicking and paddling frantically to get to shore before it devours you,*

Daphne shook her head. *Jesus, girl, you need to get it together.*

"I'd love some," he said, smiling broadly.

Huh. Wonder if he smiled like that when he quietly slipped out of my apartment like a thief, with not so much as a "see ya, wouldn't wanna be ya"?

"Hope red's okay." She reached into the cabinet for another glass and filled it for him.

"My favorite kind," he said. "I spent a half a year working at a vineyard in Italy, so I got to drink some amazing Super Tuscans at the time."

In her head, Daphne was using her fingers like hand puppets at him, mocking his braggy nonsense. *Aren't I so cool, I worked at a vineyard in Italy. I'm a veritable oenophile. Blah blah blah blah blah.* "Blah!"

Brady and Binti turned and stared at her. "Bleh? You don't like this wine, Daph?" her friend said.

Daphne shook her head clear. "Um, well, uh. I don't know what I was saying. Not 'bleh' though. Definitely not bleh. I love this wine. You know me. There's not a red out there I don't adore."

Binti squinted at her and cocked her head. "You okay?"

Hard to Get Over

Daphne clenched her teeth and allowed her lips to part in the fakest of smiles she could muster. Like the kind she did for her orthodontist after she got her braces off when he needed to take pictures for his records. The "get me out of here, stat!" smile. "I'm super, just super. Absolutely fine. Amazing in fact."

"Well, great," Brady said, rubbing his greedy little paws together again. "Let's dig in."

Binti didn't let even a moment get in the way of inhaling the bribery meal the jerkball brought, so she pulled out the plates and utensils and set them on the counter near the food. "Dig in, guys!"

"I thought you said you weren't hungry," Daphne said as Binti filled her plate.

"I wasn't. Until the best food ever showed up. It made me insta-hungry." She started making pig snorting sounds and she and Brady laughed as they carried their food to the table.

The two of them sat down and waited for Daphne, who began handwashing some dirty dishes in the sink, then moved on to the dishwasher to unload the clean ones there.

Binti clinked on her wineglass with her fork. "Uh, hello! Earth to Daphne. We're waiting for you over here. Are you not joining us?"

She shook he head. "Seems I've lost my appetite." She picked up a sponge and wiped down all the countertops, then pulled out the Windex and some paper towels to finish the job.

Her friend stood and came into the kitchen, picking up the last plate. "Are you planning to clean the toilets next? Come on, now. You have to eat. And if you have to eat, it might as well be something delicious. Here, take one of these shish kebab thingies." She placed a skewered chicken kebab on the plate. "And then this rice is really yummy. And the appetizer, of course. You *have* to try the sambosay goshti."

"Don't forget the soup!" Mr. Know-It-All piped in from his seat—at the head of the table. Like he was some kind of Lion King or something.

Binti scooped some of the aush soup into a bowl and carried her friend's dishes to the table. She then went back and locked arms with Daphne and led her to join them. "I kept this seat warm just for you." She pointed at the chair that naturally had to be next to the poseur. Not only was she now stuck next to him but, since he sat at the head of the table, she had to actually look at him. Great.

Binti kept glancing at Daphne and nodding at her, encouraging her to take bites like a toddler. Next thing she knew Binti would be chanting "here comes the airplane" as she tried to force food into her piehole. "See, isn't that amazing?" she said after Daphne finally sucked it up and bit into the appetizer. "It's almost like an egg roll, Afghani-style."

Daphne pursed her lips and acted as if she were eating slug entrails. But then she took another bite. And another bite. And then took a spoonful of soup.

"See, not so bad, right?" her friend said.

Daphne allowed a half smile to pierce her frown.

"Right? You can admit it. It'll be our secret." Binti curled up her napkin and threw it across the table, hitting Daphne in the forehead.

"Okay, fine, it's not half bad." She wasn't going to exactly wax eloquent about it, if that's what they were looking for. But in truth, it was delicious. And when they weren't looking, she was going to nab seconds. That is if Pig Man didn't gobble them all up, being that he'd already retreated to the kitchen for round two.

"Just goes to show you," Brady said as he seated himself again. "Sometimes the thing you think you hate the most ends up being something you learn to like."

Hard to Get Over

Daphne took Binti's balled-up napkin, scrunched it hard, and lobbed it right at Brady's head. "Don't get your hopes up, or you'll be sorely disappointed."

The last thing she planned to do was devour a heaping helping of "I told you so" from the likes of Brady McGovern.

Chapter Six

"SO, Brady, what exactly is your connection to my good friend here?"

Brady couldn't believe it had taken this long for Binti to ask that. He didn't get the impression she was hep to whatever bad blood was coursing through the veins of her good buddy.

They were sitting on the sofa, drinking wine. The cute dog had curled up next to Brady, so he petted her soft ears while he talked.

"Well, Violet left part of this place to me," he said, not sure how far into the weeds he wanted to get with his explanation. Did Binti know about how he'd ditched Daphne back in college? Probably not, or she'd have no doubt girl-ganged up on him. And while he wasn't too proud of his "hell hath no fury" line from last night, it had been impossible to not say it. 'Cause it was true. And two women going after him would be even worse. Of course, Daphne had good reason to be pissed. But he didn't want to deal with that right now. He wanted to focus on the business at hand.

"What he's omitting is that Mr. Magnanimous-Make-Nice-and-Bring-Dinner-Over here, was what's known in the business as a bang-and-run practitioner."

He blanched. She wasn't going there, was she? To think things had been going so well this evening.

Binti blurted out a laugh, nearly spitting her wine all over the sofa. "Wha—?"

"Yeah. So, long story, super short, turns out we dated in college. We had sex the night we graduated, many times, as a matter of fact. I would have even said we'd made love, except in hindsight it was obviously nothing but sex—lousy sex at that, if you know what I mean." She held up her thumb and forefinger about an inch apart, winking at Binti for emphasis. "Then he disappeared. Never heard from him again. Till now. And he wants to sell my home out from under me. The end."

"Whoa." Binti took a sip of wine. "What do you have to say about this?" She looked at Brady, whose eyes had grown wide and who probably looked like he wanted to slip out the nearest exit. He wasn't sure which bothered him more—her general accosting of him, or her implying that he had a little dick. Which, to set the record straight, was a total fallacy. Make that a *phallicsy*. He couldn't believe he was making up jokes in his mind about such a serious matter.

"It's complicated," he said at last.

"Complicated? Are you freaking joking?"

Brady looked to where the loud voice had come from, only to see Daphne's eyes closed as she muttered something that sounded like an incantation to herself. It involved a butterfly and an ocean and a shark fin, if he wasn't mistaken.

Binti held up her hands like a traffic cop trying to keep cars from plowing into the intersection after the lights stop working. "Okay, so let's start this again. So, Brady, you've got some interest in Violet's house, I gather. And Daphne, you, too, have some interest in Violet's house. So, what you have in common is Violet, amiright? And Daphne, you have a whole house of Violet's stuff you need to go through. And Brady, it sounds like it would be helpful for you to know Violet a bit better, yes?"

They both stared at Binti, Brady twirling Tortellini's ear with his finger, and Daphne speed-drinking her recently refilled glass of wine in three quick gulps.

"So I propose that you both get to work going through Violet's things. It will give you each a chance to become reacquainted, maybe bury the hatchet, Daphne, and not in any flesh. And it will serve to make some headway in the house. 'Cause girlfriend, not gonna lie, you've got a shit ton of work to do in that place before you can do anything with it. We loved Violet, but she was not a fan of throwing anything out, was she?"

Brady could see Daphne making some subtle slicing motion across her throat, no doubt trying to throw Binti off this idea. But he liked it. Digging through a lifetime of Violet's things to learn exactly who his benefactress was sounded kind of interesting.

Daphne stuck her finger up as if to make a point but Binti, who clearly had an assertive streak a mile wide, kept telling her to "zip it." Amazingly, she obliged.

Before he knew it, Binti had gotten an agreement from Daphne for her to meet him inside Violet's place at eight sharp. Who knew that feeding a frenemy's BFF some tasty food could lead to an even better outcome than he'd ever thought possible? This was going to be interesting. Or dangerous. Time would tell.

Brady's sleep was whacked and he was lucky if he'd slept three hours the whole night. Jet lag was torture. And he needed coffee, badly. After googling a decent bakery nearby, one that would serve basic black coffee while supporting the mainlining of some much-needed sugar, he Ubered there. He picked up a selection of pastries and two black coffees while his driver waited and returned just shy of eight. He wondered if Daphne would even honor her commitment. If not, what was he going to do? Sit in the rubble of this old gal's life, twiddling his thumbs? Or hire a lawyer to take care of whatever and skip town? Again. As tempting as that notion was, no way could he do that. It would only reinforce to her what an asshole he was. And he had been an asshole. Didn't mean he was one now. He'd done a lot of growing up over the years, some of it forced on him due to circumstances beyond his control. Like his parents' deaths.

At five after eight, he heard a barely discernable sound at the door. He wouldn't accuse it of being an actual knock—more like an accidental meeting of knuckle against wood, once, twice, then a third time.

Brady opened the door and thrust the to-go cup of coffee into Daphne's hand. "Here. Figured the way you were downing that wine last night, you might need this."

She glared at him. "I wouldn't have had to down wine like it was water were it not for your unwelcome presence."

Deciding to ignore that comment, he got down to business. "So, I took the liberty of researching how to go through a stranger's things—"

"You actually researched that?" She rolled her eyes and shook her head. "Who does that?"

He side-eyed her. "Well, someone tasked with doing that, of course."

"That is the weirdest thing I've ever heard."

"I'm sure you've heard far stranger things in your life."

"Yeah, like the sound of you pretending you liked me."

Brady glanced around the living room and spread his hands out wide. "Well, looks like we've got our work cut out for us. I think we divide our piles into three things: keep, donate, and throw out."

Daphne heaved a sigh. "You forgot an important one: sell. Or does that not matter to you since they're not yours to sell?"

"You sound awfully anxious to profit off of Aunt Violet's life." He knew that was a low blow and regretted the words the minute they passed his lips. He held up his hands to erase them. "I'm sorry. I didn't mean that. Let's forget I even said it."

She glared at him through slitted eyes and poked her finger into his chest. "Fine. But understand this, Brady McGovern: I'm in charge here. Everything—and I mean everything, right down to a mousetrap or an ant motel—has to be cleared through me before it gets trashed. You got it?"

Boy, Daphne sure had turned surly in her old age. He held up his hands in defeat. "Whatever. Just point me where to go and tell me what to do." He shoved the bag of pastries in front of her. "By the way, here's your breakfast."

Chapter Seven

AWWW, man.

Every time Daphne thought she could one-up Brady with a zinger of some sort, he'd swoop in with an unwelcome kind gesture to make her feel like a complete heel for being a complete heel. Which she knew she was being, yet somehow she couldn't help herself.

It was against her better judgment, but she was hungry, so she took a bite of the flaky, buttery, French onion croissant he'd gotten her. How had he known she'd want such an unusual type of croissant? Not as if she'd ever eaten something like that around him—she'd never even seen a French onion croissant before. Though she always did go to obscene lengths for a good French onion soup... Maybe he remembered that? But why would he remember something like that about someone he didn't even care about?

She took a bite and it was so sublime her eyes rolled back in her head. Who knew a specialty croissant could be better than sex? Not that she would even remember how good sex was at this point; it had been so damned long. She'd given up even bothering to find someone she might want to consider doing it with. Nowadays between the shallow men you had to swipe through on dating apps and the fact that every guy on the planet was so hooked on internet porn there was no way to meet their expectations, it all seemed a moot point. So it was official: she would stick to caramelized onion on a croissant instead. She woke from her reverie to realize she'd been moaning while eating the thing. *Moaning.* God, what was wrong with her? She glanced over to see Brady staring at her with a knowing grin pasted on his face.

"What?" she said, furling her brow.

He cocked his head. "Oh, nothing." He stuck both hands in his pockets and she glanced down at the most inopportune moment to notice that he'd suddenly sprung a bulge in his shorts.

"God," she said, pointing at his crotch. "You men are so Pavlovian. How does someone merely eating a pastry get you hot and bothered?"

"First off, it wasn't the pastry-eating that caused that autonomic response, thanks. It was the sound of you moaning as if you were in the throes of an orgasm. And yes, the sound of an orgasm is all it takes for a guy to get a hard-on." He shook his head. "And the other thing is maybe it was just my body's way of proving your lie from last night."

She frowned. "My lie? I didn't lie about anything."

He held up his hand, spreading his thumb and pointer finger apart about an inch. "This ring a bell?"

She smiled. "Heh. Well, yeah, so?"

"So what if I wanted to ask Binti out on a date? Now she wouldn't even go, because she thinks I'm diminutive."

"Diminutive? Is that what they call it?" She walked farther into the living room and began shifting piles of stuff to make a clearing in the center of the room. "Besides, you can't date my best friend."

"Why not?"

"Because you're you," she huffed. "What you did to me permanently disqualifies you from being with anyone I know or love. You screw me, you screw them."

Hard to Get Over

He held his hands up in surrender. "Okay, okay, fine. I will never date anyone you know, have known, will ever know. But at least clarify that I've got a big cock, would you? It's the least you could do, having ripped into my reputation."

Ugh, the mere mention of that big cock of his had things stirring in parts that she thought had fossilized. She crossed her legs against the sensations now supercharging her clit. It was undeniable: he had an award-winning penis and knew how to use it. But she couldn't let on to him that she remembered it. Badgering him the way she had about something that happened long ago was so unlike her. But under the circumstances, it was too easy to do, and she felt validated for having the chance stick it to him. It was the least she could do.

"Honey, you ruined your own reputation when you walked out on me."

He rolled his eyes and pretended to buff his nails. "Whatever. I guess I can show Binti when the time is right that you were a hundred percent wrong about me."

"You mean about your girth, or your worth?" *Oh, snap. That was a good comeback.*

He surprised her by bursting into laughter. "Oh, Daphne, I remember you always had a great sense of humor."

Well, then why did you up and blow me off like you did?

She decided not to continue the discussion and instead rerouted them toward the business at hand. "Enough chitchat. It's time to get down to business. I'm going to start in this corner." She pointed toward the window end of the living room on the right. "And you're going to be across from me, there." He got defaulted to the corner on the left. She wanted to keep him close by to ensure he didn't throw out anything of value—emotional or financial. "I am going to grab some sheets from the closet, and we will make piles on each sheet for the appropriate way of dispensing of things. Now if there is a legitimate piece of trash, you can clear it with me before throwing it in the garbage. Got it?"

"Yes, sire. At your service, sire."

She lifted an eyebrow and turned around without comment, not even asking him why the grandfather clock was covered in tablecloths.

They fell into silence for a while as they worked. Daphne figured it would be awkward. but she got so caught up in memories that she almost forgot The Jerk was even in the room. It was easy to purge piles of old magazines and things that almost no one would want. But the sentimental things were tough. She picked up Violet's favorite sweater—a snagged, old blue cardigan—and held it to her face, sobbing quietly.

"Everything okay over there?" Brady said.

She peered from around the sweater and wiped away her tears with her T-shirt.

"Do you normally cry over outerwear?"

"Stop," she said. "It was Violet's favorite sweater. I think her sister knitted it for her years ago. She wore it all the time, especially after her sister died. It was kind of a touchstone to the past for her. I can barely think of Violet without thinking about this sweater draped over her shoulders."

Brady was silent for a beat.

"I'm sorry." Standing, he looked around till he spotted a box of tissues and carried it over to Daphne. "Here."

She was shocked that he had the capacity to have feelings. Which wasn't very charitable of her. Plenty of people had the capacity to have feelings even if they'd done cruel things too. It was the human condition, wasn't it?

"Thanks," she said, smiling weakly. "Every now and then it hits me in weird ways. Like in the afternoon, at five o'clock, when she and I would sit down with a cup of tea and talk about the day. I miss that so much."

"She sounds like a nice lady."

"You don't know the half of it. Violet was something special. So sweet and thoughtful and joyful. She used to sit on the porch and wave to everyone who walked by." She flailed her arms like she was Violet on the porch waving. "Half the time she'd insist they stop and talk to her. Or she'd offer them a brownie or a cookie. Violet loved her sweets. She made the most delicious shortbread I've ever had. I never did get the recipe from her. I guess I always figured I'd have her to make it for me."

Tears filled her eyes again.

"I'm sorry, Daph. I know she was special to you." Brady came over and sat next to her and put his arm around her.

"She was like a grandma and a mom and a good friend all wrapped up in one to me," she said, her voice trembling. "I miss her so much."

She tried to hold back her sobs but it wasn't working and pretty soon she was ugly-crying, which was the worst. She sounded like a goose in heat. If geese went into heat. She wondered if that was even a thing. Maybe they just laid eggs. No, that would be like immaculate conception. Impossible. There had to be a boy goose in there somewhere. She remembered watching a video about how horribly violent male ducks are, forcing their ugly duck selves on poor, unsuspecting girl ducks who are going about their business, tooling around the lake. What was it with the males in the world? Did they merely do whatever they wanted, when they wanted, and to hell with the females? Was it even fair to wonder about that? It's not like all males were awful. Well, certainly male ducks. At least from what she saw on that YouTube video. She shuddered. It was pretty awful. She was glad she wasn't a girl duck.

Wait a second. Was that Brady reaching around to give her a hug? And was she supposed to hug back? Wasn't that proper hug protocol? When someone is comforting you in your time of need with a hug, you reciprocate the gesture, right? And what about when he's running his fingers through your (very tangled) curls? And dragging his fingertips along your scalp in that way that made you mew like a satiated kitten when he did that all those years ago. Because that was what he was suddenly doing. At eight thirty in the morning in Violet's living room while they sifted through her life. And why did it make her into that very Pavlovian dog she'd accused him of being, because she was suddenly feeling all sorts of tingly in her long-neglected girl parts. Was this because she hadn't been touched by another man in, like, forever? She'd truly forgotten how sensual the touch of another human could be.

She decided the appropriate course of action was to relent, to simply ride the horse in the direction it was galloping and hug him back. After all, he was being kind enough to either care or at least approximate a degree of caring. That had to count for something.

But then he doubled down, pressing her head to his shoulder, his hand flattened to the back of her head as he intermittently stroked her from the top of her scalp to the bottom of it. And she couldn't help but melt into him, just as the years suddenly melted away and they were back in her apartment all those years ago. And she remembered why she'd felt so safe in his arms: they were warm and secure and caring.

Hard to Get Over

But how could she reconcile this Brady with that Brady and stop hating him so intensely?

Chapter Eight

WHAT a difference a day made. Was it just a little more than twenty-four hours ago that Daphne was a full-on raging Medusa toward him? And now here they were in a lover's clinch of sorts—albeit one rooted in her sadness, not lust, but still. This was progress. It's not like he had some grand scheme to seduce her, but now that he held her in his arms, he was starting to remember the old Daphne, the sweet girl he met on the first day of their senior symposium during their last semester of college. He'd been so impressed with her smart questions and the way she carried herself with such confidence. She seemed so much more mature than the other girls he'd dated: smart and ambitious and not willing to take no for an answer. It didn't hurt that she showed up at the lecture in her workout clothes—usually a tiny sports bra and a pair of yoga pants. Those outfits left little to his imagination, which ran rampant even when he merely looked at her rack.

They'd hit it off immediately. Their casual banter alone was so sexy, it nearly got him hard remembering it. He hadn't realized what a turn-on a smart woman was until she came along and now he wondered why he'd found her so easy to cast aside. They'd gone from casually chatting before and after their lectures to dating pretty exclusively within a couple of weeks. So maybe it was unfair for him to act as if they'd barely dated at all. It had been nearly six months by the time he bailed on her. Granted he'd tried to tell her what he had planned. But she never wanted to hear it. So, he'd stopped discussing it. It was far easier to talk the language they spoke best, in bed. And there they had no disagreements, ever.

As he stroked Daphne's hair, he couldn't help but nudge his face toward hers, till their lips were almost touching. He turned a little bit more and pressed his forehead to hers. Daphne had stopped crying, and the only thing he could hear was their breathing, twined together. And the damned grandfather clock ticking away. He slid his hands around to cup her face and angled his head, settling his lips on hers. His breath hitched in his chest as a flood of memories washed over him, the soft warmth of her mouth on his, the sweet bite of the cinnamon gum she always kept tucked away in her mouth, the soft coo wafting up from her throat, all of it bringing him back to those simpler times when they hadn't a care in the world.

At first it was all him, as he slowly slipped his tongue into her mouth, probing, exploring, searching, trying to elicit a response from her. He grew discouraged, worried she wasn't going to reciprocate, but then he heard the moan rising from her throat and felt her tongue warm against his as they tangled and explored each other's mouths. Brady pulled her tighter toward him as one hand slipped lower and settled briefly on her waist before beginning to explore, inching beneath her tank top till it found her bra. Luckily it was one of those thin ones, not all padded and wired, so he could feel the shape of her breast and trace the outline of her hardening nipple. God, he didn't want to rush this, but how could he not? His fingers pressed beneath the lower edge of the bra, pushing it up and over her breast, and finally—*finally!*—he felt the warmth of her flesh, the curve of her beautiful breast, the hard press of her swollen nipple against his fingers.

Daphne moaned again, and he took that as a green light, moving his other hand along her body as he leaned forward to ease her onto Violet's oriental rug, giving him easier access and enabling him to slip his fingers beneath the waistband of her shorts as she thrust her hips toward his probing hand. With ease, his fingers slid beneath her panties, quickly parting her lips and finding her slick and ready. He groaned into her mouth and she cried out at his touch.

"Is this okay?" He knew he had to at least ask.

"More," she said, pressing her pelvis toward him. "Please. More."

The man was honor bound to continue, immersing his fingers in her moist juices, then plunging into her center as she pulsed against him, encouraging him on. Meanwhile his other hand massaged her breast, tweaking her nipple with his thumb and forefinger, causing her to moan even more. Every note of her voice was going straight to his dick, which strained the seams of his shorts at this point. He'd have liked nothing more than to strip off his clothes and quickly bury his hard cock into her wet center but knew he'd have to take it slow, or else this scared filly would hop the fence and run away in no time flat. At long last, he broke their kiss, only to trail his lips from her mouth, along her chin, and down her neck. Tracing his tongue down to her nipples, he laved first one, then the other, then nipped them with his teeth.

Daphne's hips continued thrusting faster and faster against his hands as he fingered her, alternating swirling his fingers around her clit and plunging them into her dripping channel.

"Come for me, Daph," he murmured against her nipple as he drew it into his mouth to suckle. "I want to feel you come around my fingers."

Hard to Get Over

She squirmed against him, her body searching for her climax as he sucked and pinched and pulled her nipples and pumped his fingers inside her as if his hand were his cock. If only. Then she let out a piercing wail as her pussy spasmed against his slick fingers and her body twitched with the intensity of her orgasm.

Finally the icebreaker he'd been looking for. Surely Daphne would finally warm up to him after that powerful stress reliever.

Chapter Nine

DAPHNE lay there catching her breath, panting hard, when the clock struck ten. And only then did she awaken from her lust-soaked stupor to realize that she was just finger-fucked by her traitorous ex on the living room carpet of her dear departed neighbor Violet. Good God, what would Violet think of her? And what was she supposed to do now? And holy shit, did that feel amazing. If only she could do that at least once a day, life would be so much more relaxing. She could even stop meditating. A good orgasm was worth way more for your mental health than a dinky little meditation session.

Nevertheless, right now she was lying on the floor of Violet's home, her ex's fingers resting on her very sensitive clitoris, his face pressed against her hard nipple. Talk about awkward. Yet awesome. Yet super, super awkward. 'Cause she so could not have this happen with Brady. She needed to keep this all aboveboard and professional and completely void of bodily fluids of any kind. Even if said fluids did help her achieve the best—and only—orgasm she'd had in as long as she could remember.

She didn't dare open her eyes, as if that would make it more real than it actually was. And suddenly she could feel Brady's mouth work its way toward her mouth and his tongue once again slip, unimpeded, past her betraying lips. What was she to do but participate? It felt so, well, so right. That was the problem: something so wrong felt so damned right. But never could anything sexual with Brady McGovern feel right. He was so off-limits he was practically on-limits. She had to bring this debacle to a stop, immediately. She slid her hands up, accidentally bumping into the telltale bulge in his shorts—yowza, she was pretty sure that wasn't a banana in his pocket. Her hands pulled away like she'd touched a hot stove. And he was too hot to touch. If she dared even go there, it would be so far down a rabbit hole of lust that they'd need to send in a search and rescue team to save her. Instead, she used her hands to push against his chest, even as he was pulling her closer, spreading tender kisses on her forehead, her cheeks, her chin. It all felt so soft and warm and loving. But she knew better.

"Uh, er, um, well, I hate to say it but that was a big mistake," she said as she squirmed away from his reach. "I mean, well—"

"Mistake?" Brady raked his fingers through his hair and closed his eyes. "That was anything but a mistake, Daph. That was amazing."

"It's just that, well, I mean sure, it was amazing on one level, but—"

"No buts, Daphne, it felt good. It was downright revelatory."

Ugh. She hated that he was right. It *was* revelatory, in that it showed her how badly she needed to sex up her celibate life, big time. How could she have gone so long without *that?* But with him? Why would she do that to herself? She knew his record, and it wasn't a shining example of what she wanted from a man in her life. She wanted stability, trust, reliability. He was the opposite of all that.

"Yes, but no."

"Yes but no?" He grabbed her hand, his fingers sticky with her juices, which was such a turn-on. At that moment she wanted nothing more than a command performance, stat.

"This is so wrong," she said.

"Only if you make it that way." He pulled her toward him. "I'm here, you're here, we're working toward a common goal, we have a past—"

"Uh, hello, not a stellar one."

"It was till it wasn't."

"In a big way."

"I was young and selfish and didn't use my head to think about you. I'm not that boy now. I'm a different man."

Daphne heaved a sigh. She was so not interested in anything more than sex with Brady. But then again, what would be wrong with a little dalliance? This thing they were caught up with was a temporary happening. What would be the problem with taking advantage of him—someone she knew intimately already, someone who could, well, for lack of a better word, service her? Daphne needed some servicing at this point. Someone to get her back into fighting shape. One thing this orgasm taught her was that being trapped in a sexual dry spell meant she'd been missing out in a big way. It would be better for her to do it with a known commodity rather than swiping left—or was it right?—to find some stranger she might end up sleeping with. 'Cause ugh, she didn't want to get intimate with a stranger. And here, now, she had her very own boy toy on hand to use to her advantage, which seemed downright brilliant.

"Daphne, hear me out," Brady started to say. "I know neither of us expected this to happen, but now that it has, it would be a crime to nip it in the bud. Our bodies know each other. We have muscle memory together. Think how much fun this could be."

Hard to Get Over

Daphne bit her lip as she pondered her options. Lying on the floor with her pants pushed down and her shirt pushed up, exposing her breasts, was probably not the best way to do this. It could lead her to make a rash decision. She looked at Brady, the outline of his cock still pressing against his shorts. And yeah, she'd lied. It was not a teeny weenie. She remembered it as being quite generous in every way, and it might be fun to reacquaint herself with his best feature sometime. Besides, the rest of him was not too shabby either. He'd only gotten better-looking with age. And his body was in great shape. It seemed a shame to waste all that good manliness.

"Okay, fine. So, here's the deal," she said, turning onto her side to look him in the eyes. "The only reason I'm agreeing to this"—she pointed back and forth at him and herself and twined her fingers together symbolically—"is because I've been desperately deprived of this for too damned long. And it felt really fucking good. So, I'll agree to a little, shall we say, dalliance, but on my terms: when I say so and until I say we're done. I'm calling the shots now, and I will maintain control of what goes on. Deal?"

Chapter Ten

BRADY gulped. The lady drove a hard bargain. But right now, if it was between a bad case of the blue balls threatening to require amputation and pretty much any nonnegotiable terms to allow him to advance the troops, he was all in.

"Okay," he said. "I'm at your mercy, your highness."

"Good," she said, pulling her shorts up and tugging her shirt back down. "And now it's time to get back to work."

Well, fuck. She certainly had him by the figurative balls. He needed to get off so badly he would give the damned house away in exchange for her whacking him off. Or better yet riding him like a bronco till he shot his cum deep inside her. Though he knew beggars couldn't be choosers.

He squinted at her. "You sure you don't want to pick up where we left off? Kind of finish what we started?"

She grinned. "I feel pretty damned complete, thanks."

He frowned. "Yeah but, well…" He glanced down at his crotch, which was starting to wither with the knowledge that his dick was not going to get an invitation to come out to play. He then fixed his gaze on her.

"Ahhh, you mean you want me to…" She pointed at herself, then at his dick, and shrugged.

He nodded, trying to maintain hope in the face of despair. "That's generally the idea. Usually, a gentleman will pleasure his woman first, and then she returns the favor. Sometimes it's with her hands. Other times—if you're lucky—it's with her mouth, or even better yet, with her steamy, glistening, swollen pussy. I prefer the latter, when she sits on top of it and gyrates around." He hoped this dirty talk was stirring her up a bit, maybe tipping the balance in his favor.

She scratched her chin as if she was thinking. He knew she was dicking on him. "Gotcha. But right now, we need to get back to work, 'kay?"

She stood up, walked back to her corner of the room, and began sorting items as if nothing out of the ordinary had transpired.

Shit, she was being a ballbuster. Literally. But he probably deserved it. So, he delicately rearranged his junk and stood up. "If you'll forgive me, I need a minute to reconnoiter."

"Okay, but don't be long!" She winked at him.

Oh, there would be hell to pay down the road for this… as soon as he could get the upper hand. In the meantime, his hand was going to be busy in the bathroom, taking care of necessary business.

After excusing himself to the second-floor bathroom, Brady rifled around in the cabinets till he could find some lotion. This was an all-hands-on-deck situation. He had to jack off or he'd be unable to continue working downstairs. He'd come so close to going for round two, but that didn't seem in the offing right now. Only if and when she'd permit it. Fuck.

Brady dropped his shorts and boxer briefs and squirted the lotion into his hand—what better use for hand lotion than this?—and circled his somewhat stiff cock with his fingers, smoothing the lubricant around as he pulled and twisted with his hand, first slowly, then more quickly. He only had to think about Daphne's slick pussy to stiffen his dick even more and imagine her gorgeous tits bared for his eyes only, her hard nipples in his mouth. His balls tightened and a tingly sensation stirred in his groin. God how he wanted to ram himself deep into her wet pussy, her legs spread wide so he could watch the slide and pull of his hardened cock, her swollen lips swallowing him up. As he trembled, his cock erupted in spurt after spurt, till he was spent with the effort. He sat on the edge of the tub, waiting to gather enough strength to clean up after himself and get back downstairs. He should've been angry that she refused to reciprocate, but for some reason it only served to amuse him. He loved to play sexual games and felt confident he would, ultimately, prevail in this game of cat and mouse.

At last, he returned to the living room, wishing he'd taken a ten-minute nap first, 'cause the exertion had drained him of energy.

"Everything okay?" she said, suppressing a laugh. That little witch! She knew what he was doing upstairs. But he was cool with that. He'd get the last laugh even though it might take some time. And hopefully it would involve her seated on his cock, exactly like he'd imagined.

Chapter Eleven

DID Daphne feel like a bit of a jerk for having sent Brady off to masturbate when she could have easily enjoyed taking care of him herself? Nah. It was fun exacting a tiny bit of good-hearted revenge on the guy. Sure, a lot of years had passed since he'd left her heartbroken and humiliated, but this? It was better than therapy in helping her get that whole experience out of her system.

The next couple of hours they settled in quietly to sort and purge. Occasionally Brady would try to throw something away that Daphne would freak out about, sometimes a little irrationally.

"But they're ticket stubs to some show at the Kennedy Center, Daph," he said. "Who needs that, ever, anywhere?"

"Except it was when Violet took me to see *Hamilton*," she said. "It was such a treat and so special. We had cocktails on the terrace at intermission and sang songs from the show." She sighed. Clearly Brady was getting exasperated with this stuff.

"How are you ever going to purge all the stuff in this house if you can't even throw away a ticket stub?" He pinched the bridge of his nose, a sure sign of annoyance.

"Sorry. I can't forget about that date."

"Okay, I have an idea. What say you take a picture of the ticket stub. That way you always have it to look back on, but the actual stub no longer causes unnecessary clutter. Can you live with that?"

Daphne lifted her brow. That was awfully reasonable. She needed to concede something. "Okay, fine." She held up the stub in front of her face and took a selfie. She knew it was silly but it made her feel better.

At some point in the afternoon, they happened upon a big box of photographs.

"Whoa, I love old pictures," she said. "So interesting to see the old styles of fashion and home décor."

"Do you know anyone in any of the pictures?"

"Does that matter?"

"Well, sorta," he said. "What's the point of keeping a huge box of pictures of complete strangers?"

"But they belonged to Violet. It feels dishonorable to throw them in the trash."

"Believe it or not, you can give them away to flea markets. There is a huge market for old photographs. Someone will find them and buy them and do something cool with them. That would make Violet happy to have her family photographs repurposed."

She pursed her lips. "Huh. How do you know that's even a thing?"

Brady heaved a sigh. "Just something I had to do one time." He quickly changed the subject. "I have an idea. How about I hold up the picture and you tell me if it's something to keep or give away? You take two seconds per picture and we'll make a game of it, okay?"

"Fine, but I'm making no promises."

For the first half hour or so they were able to make a sizable pile of giveaways. But then midway down in the box, Brady found something and froze in his place.

Hard to Get Over

Daphne looked up. "Everything okay?" He'd lost color in his face.

She reached over, pulled the photographs from his hands, and studied them closely. "Is there someone in these pictures you know?" She knew he had some distant relationship to Violet, so it was possible.

"Can you give me a minute?"

She frowned. "Yeah. Sure."

Brady got up and walked toward the kitchen. He didn't even know where to go. Spotting a door, he opened it and it led him onto a nice deck that backed up to some woods. On it were a long sofa and a couple of lounge chairs with thick cushions. Tall, latticed screens covered with clematis vines and flowers provided a privacy buffer on either side. Window boxes filled with flowers lined the railings of the deck, which extended to both sides of the duplex. Huh, interesting. So this was a shared space for both Violet and Daphne.

Brady lay down on the sofa and closed his eyes. The last thing he'd expected was to see a picture of his parents. At their wedding. Now, at least, he knew Violet was a close enough relative to have attended his folks' wedding. They looked so young and hopeful. They had no idea they'd die too young. And leave him holding the bag, the sole survivor, no family to speak of.

Those photos threw him for a loop. He thought he'd put the past behind him, mostly by not thinking about his folks. If he did think about them, he knew a well of sadness would overtake him and that was the last thing he wanted to deal with.

Especially now. A sound prompted him to look up to see hummingbirds feeding from flowers in the window boxes. It was soothing to watch those tiny creatures with their hearts beating a mile a minute. How they stayed still in midair while they drank the nectar was incredible. As he stared ahead at some birds perched in a bird feeder, a crow cawed from a nearby tree.

He nodded off for a little while, only to be stirred awake by Daphne.

"Hey," she said, tapping his arm. "You all right?"

He sat up, shook the cobwebs from his head, and invited her to sit next to him.

"You ready to talk about it?"

Ugh, he totally didn't want to discuss his dead parents. But he needed to share this with her. Otherwise, it would simply hang there, making things uncomfortable.

He sighed. "So, a few years into my itinerant life, I'd recently finished hiking the tallest mountain in every state in the country. It took me two years. I was kind of jazzed with my accomplishment. But then I got a call—the call no one ever wants to get—and learned my folks had died in a small plane crash."

Daphne's eyes grew wide and she covered her mouth with her hand. "Oh, Brady, I had no idea. I'm so sorry." She reached over and placed her hands over his.

God, he hated everything about this revelation when he had to share it, but he detested the pity the most. Inevitably, everyone he told would get that same look: their brows would furrow, a look of horror would cross their faces, they'd not know what to say, and then it would be awkward. There was no comfortable way to share this sort of news.

He nodded to Daphne. "Thanks, I appreciate it."

Hard to Get Over

"And what happened inside, a little while ago, when you were going over the photographs?"

He shook his head. "Believe it or not, those pictures I came upon were of my parents. Violet knew my parents well enough to have been at my Mom and Dad's wedding." He shrugged. "I guess it threw me off. The last thing I expected to encounter. And the thing is, I usually feel like I'm past that, you know?"

She shook her head. "No, I don't know. I don't think anyone ever gets over the loss of their parents. I mean, they're your parents. They were the foundation of your life, right?"

"Sure. Of course. But maybe I'm good at compartmentalizing—"

"You *are* a guy, after all." She winked.

"Yeah, one of our less admirable skills. Or more admirable, as the case may be. Anyhow, I felt as if I'd gotten past it. I mean, it was hard. I don't have any brothers or sisters. Or aunts and uncles, for that matter. I take that back. There is one uncle somewhere, my dad's brother, but he went off the rails at some point, and I couldn't even begin to tell you where he is. Never tracked him down for the funeral."

"Oh, Brady, did you have to plan your own parents' funerals?"

He frowned and nodded.

"And no one to help you?"

"My dad was career military, so they moved around all the time. But my mother had her core group of ladies—they all propped each other up throughout the ups and downs of that kind of lifestyle—and Mom's posse helped tremendously. I was still in so much shock. And then afterward, there was so much to do: settling their affairs, closing up the house and cleaning it up and purging their lives, basically, then selling it."

"Your childhood home?"

He shook his head. "Nah. We never had such a thing moving around like we did. But it was the last home I knew."

"Still, a home base that you lost."

He arched his brow at her. "You of all people should know I'm not one to keep a home base."

"'Tis a shame," she said, spreading her arms out wide. "Where else to store all of your accumulated shit?"

He laughed. "That is the truest statement you've made yet. A giant shit receptacle. For which you pay a bank each month for the right to dump more unnecessary shit into."

She laughed too. "Ahh, Brady. I had no idea. I'm so sorry. Here I thought you were a soulless rat bastard and now I learn you've got so much more depth to you."

"Maybe there's a little soulless rat bastard in me. I mean, I did leave you high and dry."

"In the interest of maintaining a respectable degree of empathy toward you, I'm not going to address that now."

"Thanks for your generosity of spirit." He grinned. "You aren't such a bad person yourself."

"Or maybe I'm badder than you realize."

"Prove it."

"You don't think I can?"

"Surprise me."

Chapter Twelve

DAPHNE stood and reached for the hem of her tank top, slipping it over her head. Next she shimmied out of her running shorts and stood before Brady in her bra and panties. A grin spread across his face as she knelt between his legs on the sofa, unbuttoned his shorts, and pulled them down, along with his boxer briefs. She lifted his shirt over his head, leaving him naked on the sofa. Outside. Straddling his hips, she reached down and popped the clasp of her bra, quickly discarding it. She loved that he'd grown instantly hard and felt him pressing up against her panties, the only article of clothing still left on either of them.

"You're surprising me, Daphne, stripping naked out here in the wide open where the neighbors could see. I like that about you. Exhibitionist tendencies, maybe?"

What she didn't need to tell him was that neighbors on either side were on vacation right now, and unless there were some creepers spying from the woods, their privacy was relatively assured. But that was okay. If he wanted to think people were spying, so be it.

It was brave of her to do this—Daphne had never been known as much of a risk taker. Hell, she parked herself in her little duplex and worked till bedtime most nights. Boring had become her middle name. A big risk for her would be going to a bar with Binti, and even then, she begged off more often than not. Having sex with her ex—an ex she'd been pissed at within the past twenty-four hours—was on its own way out of her comfort zone. Though she did become comfortable with it quite quickly, because, well, sex. And having sex with her ex on the deck was far beyond her norm. She was more of a sex-in-the-bedroom-with-the-lights-out kinda gal.

She rather liked the feeling of the late afternoon breeze across her bare skin, making her nipples pucker tightly. And she loved the look of pure lust in Brady's eyes as he watched her, not knowing what to expect from her. She grinned as she pinched her nipples. It was kind of fun being the seductress, especially since she'd had no intention of doing this with him. She'd planned to make him wait long and hard. Sure, she knew he'd gone upstairs this morning and rubbed one out. She loved that he was that desperate for her that he had to do that or not function. And she loved the feeling of his hard, massive cock as she rubbed herself against him right now, nothing between them but her thin panties.

"Do you want people to see us having sex, Brady?" she said as she continued to stroke herself along his cock.

He reached up and pulled her close enough to kiss, pressing his mouth to hers as if his life depended on it.

"I want to watch you get off while rubbing against me. That's what I want to see. While I suck on your gorgeous tits. Will you do that for me?"

She leaned forward so that he could squeeze her tits together, nipping first on one nipple with his teeth before latching onto the other and sucking hard. She let out a loud moan.

"Oh my God, Brady. You're killing me."

"If by killing you I'm helping you toward your goal of *la petite mort*, then by all means, let me do it."

"La petite mort?" Her high school French didn't include idioms, and as far she could remember, that translated to *the little death*. A far cry from her goal.

"It's a French expression referring to the intense physical and emotional release one experiences with an orgasm."

"The French do have a way with words."

"And with kisses." He pulled her toward him for another kiss as his hand reached down and slipped beneath her panties to stroke her.

"Oh, Brady. More."

"With pleasure," he said, adding another finger as she paused from rubbing against him to enjoy the feeling of his fingers playing with her.

Finally, she pressed down against his cock again, gyrating against him. The sensation, coupled with Brady's fingers on her, became overwhelming and she shouted "I'm coming!" as her body convulsed and she flooded his hands with her juices.

After a minute she looked down at him, realizing she'd left him hanging yet again. "I'm sorry, this was supposed to be your turn."

He grinned. "Trust me, I'm enjoying every minute of this."

"Then let me double your pleasure." She reached down and pulled aside her panties, and took hold of his cock and began to stroke it along her wet center.

"Fuck, Daphne, that is impossibly amazing. I don't think I've ever experienced a greater sensation than the tip of my cock gliding along your swollen pussy. I think I've died and gone to heaven."

"There's more where that came from. But I want you to be honest with me. How long since you've been with anyone? I need to know you're clean. 'Cause I haven't been with anyone in literally years, so I can assure you I am."

"I'm good, D. As a matter of habit, I get tested regularly and I've not been with anyone in at least six months and I've been tested more recently than that."

"You swear?"

He held up three fingers. "Scout's honor."

"In that case…" She reached between them and pressed the head of his cock to her opening and gradually slid down onto him.

"Can you experience la petite mort before you actually come?" he said. "'Cause I feel like I'm dead already with pleasure."

Daphne rocked on top of Brady, riding him like her life depended on it, clutching his cock inside her pussy and grinding into him. Lifting up, she slammed down on him again, pushing him deep inside her. She didn't know if it was from not having had sex in a long while or because this sex was that much more spiritual, but holy shit, her body was on fire with sensation.

"Oh shit, Brady, I'm going to come again," she whimpered as her body trembled and she once again felt spasms erupt in her pelvis and spread through her body. While she continued to thrust against him, Brady returned the favor and plunged in deeper, groaning loudly, filling her with his seed in pulsating wave after wave.

Daphne collapsed on top of him and they both promptly fell asleep, sated and spent. La petite mort, indeed.

Chapter Thirteen

BY the end of the week, Daphne relented and they ordered a dumpster, which now stood in front of the house. Like or not, she had to admit that Violet owned a whole lot of stuff that was of no value to anyone but Violet. And she was no longer here to treasure it.

"I get it, Daph," Brady said. "When I first started clearing out my parents' home, I was trying so hard to salvage anything that might have some sort of meaning. Like did my mother's punch bowl matter to her? I couldn't have given a shit about a big old punch bowl, but maybe it was some family treasure. I learned pretty quickly that there weren't a whole lot of things worth keeping. That's when I started taking pictures of things to make myself feel better—to create some visual representation of the 'stuff' without allowing it to weigh me down. My whole way of life has always been about not being anchored down with stuff—"

"Or people?"

He pressed his lips together. They were taking a break from the Big Purge, eating lunch on the back deck, which had become an excuse for an afternoon quickie every day this past week. Brady was perfectly happy with that. He didn't like getting into deeper conversations about himself, though, and wanted to keep it light and easy.

"It's not that I don't want to be bogged down with people." He chose his words carefully. "It's just that there is a simplicity to life when you carry your world on your back. Adding people into that mix makes things more complicated."

"Is that why you dumped me?"

"I didn't dump you, per se." He frowned. "More like I chickened out from trying to make you understand where I was coming from."

"But where you were coming from was ridiculous—wanting to leave and not come back?"

"It's what I needed to do. It wasn't anything about you, really. It was all about me. And my shortcomings, or my idiosyncrasies, or maybe because all I knew growing up was about being on my own, so I needed to find me again."

"Did you?"

"Did I what?"

"Find you. You said you needed to find you again."

He shrugged. "I guess I grew to understand myself a bit better. I learned to appreciate the world, different cultures, the fragility of our globe. I got to be a vagrant on my terms, rather than being uprooted right after getting started again. Unlike my entire childhood, when being uprooted was out of my control."

"And that was important to you?"

"More than I could have imagined. So maybe that was what I meant by finding me. Actually empowering me to make my own decisions, be my own person, not live my life at the whims of others."

"Wow, that military brat thing sure did rattle you, didn't it?"

"I guess more than I realized. I needed to break free of that world."

"So where are you now?"

Hard to Get Over

He smiled, tucking her hair behind her ear. "I'm right here, with you."

She rolled her eyes and smacked him playfully. "I know that, silly. But where are you in terms of coming or going or disappearing in the middle of the night again?"

He fixed his gaze on hers. "You know I'd never do that again, don't you? I was a boy then. I'm a man now. I honor my commitments and I own up to my intentions."

She nodded. "I'll give you a mulligan. I think that's fair and reasonable. But I still don't know what your intentions are for Violet's house—at least the part that belongs to you. I think I've made it clear to you that I want to remain here. But it's going to take cooperation from you for that to happen. I loved Violet with all my heart, but she clearly didn't think through the complications of house sharing."

"You know, in a way, I think she did," he said.

Daphne furrowed her brow. "How so?"

"Well, you and Violet shared this house in a way for many years, right?"

She nodded. "Of course. I mean, I paid her for my rent, and she had her side and I had mine. And we shared our deck."

"The deck's my favorite part."

"I bet it is." She grinned.

"I never knew what a fan I was of making love al fresco."

She cocked her head. "What'd you just say?"

"I said I am a big fan of making love al fresco."

She nodded. "Getting back to what you were saying, why do you think Violet had a plan here?"

"I think Violet had planned that you and I would share the house."

"You mean like you could rent your side out with Airbnb while you travel? And I'd stay in my side and own it straight out? And I could help maintain the property and such?"

He laughed and scratched her scalp the way she liked it. "Sounds like you've got a plan all worked out in your head there."

"Well, I was hoping you didn't need the money from the sale of Violet's home. And maybe you'd take pity on an ex-girlfriend, who kind of has her heart set on this place, both for sentimental reasons and because it's home."

"I've never put much value in the concept of home before," he said. "Home is where I put my head on my pillow at night."

"But in your case, it's not even your pillow. How can that feel like home?"

He took a bite of his sandwich. "I'm starting to understand that a bit more," he said. "Hanging out at Violet's place, I have started to appreciate things like a guaranteed warm shower. Air conditioning on a hot day. A flushing toilet."

"That's an absolute must."

"A big comfy sofa where I can cuddle up and watch TV. Basic cable, for that matter."

"Or at least streaming services," she added.

"Yup. How about a spacious kitchen counter to prepare dinners you'll share with your family and friends?"

"Now you're sounding awfully committal when you start talking about that stuff."

"Fine, how about a spacious kitchen counter you can set your lover on while you eat her instead of dinner."

Daphne blushed and tossed her napkin at him.

"What? That was the best use of a kitchen counter I could think of." He grinned. "Though I would not at all mind using it to cook a real meal, once I learn how to cook."

"And bake."

"Don't get cocky on me. One step at a time."

"One step at a time, indeed."

Chapter Fourteen

"YOU know, there's a full moon outside tonight," Daphne said. "You want to come take a look at it with me?"

"I'd love to." Brady picked up their wineglasses and the bottle and took them out back, setting them on the coffee table.

They stood side by side, looking off to where the moon was rising full and orange through the trees.

"It's beautiful, isn't it?" Daphne said. "I love looking at full moons. So mysterious and breathtaking."

"I love looking at a full moon as well, Brady said, stepping back and admiring Daphne from behind.

"You little pervert," she said, giggling. She was joking though; she loved that he stared at her body often. She loved feeling desired.

Brady came up behind her, wrapped his arms around her, flattening his hands over her tits, and nuzzled her neck.

"I didn't know a full moon could get you so horny, Mr. McGovern." She reached around and squeezed his butt, pulling him closer to her behind. She could feel his cock hardening in his pants.

"This full moon might give me a permanent erection," he said, lifting her dress and pulling her panties down to her ankles. Unbuttoning his pants, he unzipped them and lowered them and his boxer briefs enough to pull his cock out. "Now bend over and spread your legs for me."

"Don't you even say please?"

"Please, bend over now before I come all over your pretty ass."

"I aim to please." She lifted her dress to give him a perfect view of her butt. He rubbed his fingers along her seam, dipping inside to spread the juices that had already seeped out of her.

"Fuck, you get so wet."

"You make me that way."

"Good, 'cause I need to fill you with my cock."

He spread her lips and guided his cock inside her channel, and they gasped as he plunged as deep as he could go.

"Fuck me, Brady."

"I aim to please as well." With that, he slipped his cock most of the way out then thrust it back in again. He reached around and played with her clit, making her breath come at a rapid clip. Pounding deep inside her, he slipped a hand up the front of her dress to play with her nipples. "God, I want to be everywhere on you, in you. I just can't get enough of you D."

He pinched her nipple and slicked his fingers across her lips, rubbing faster as he pumped his cock in rhythm with his fingers.

"Right there, Brady, right there—" She came hard, her pussy spasming around his cock and sending him over the edge only seconds later as he filled her with his semen.

Life didn't get any better than this.

Hard to Get Over

"So you know when you mentioned earlier about how much you love the back deck—*our* back deck? Something about how much you love making love al fresco?"

They were in Daphne's house, curled up together in bed, drifting off to sleep.

He nodded, nuzzling her neck. "I really do, you know?"

"Me too, though we're going to have to be a little more circumspect when the neighbors return from holiday."

"But what about your exhibitionist tendencies?"

She laughed. "You are insane, you know that?"

"What was it you wanted to know about my comment, D?"

"It's just that, well, any time I ever thought about you and me from back then, I could never refer to us as having made love. It was always 'we had sex.' But now it feels different to me. I guess back then we were so young, we weren't mature enough to view it quite that way. But now that we've got some years under our belts, I think we recognize that what we are developing here is more than that."

He reached for her hands and wove his fingers in between hers. "I agree. What we have now, what we're in the early stages of, is something much, much more than that young lust. Don't get me wrong, nothing bad about lust. But you can't build a long-term relationship with lust alone. And speaking of building." He reached for the nightstand and took a swig of water. "Here's what I can envision. Bear with me, though, because some of this might be a little premature. I'm going with my gut, and I don't want to scare you off."

Daphne leaned forward and swirled her fingers through Brady's chest hair as he gathered his thoughts. She still could not get over the fact that she had spent the past week making love—there, she said it—with Brady McGovern of all people. It was like a dream.

"When my parents passed away, they left me financially set for life," he said. "Which was one of the reasons I kept on traveling. I could afford to. I had nowhere I had to be. And traveling afforded me the chance to keep running from my demons."

"Fair enough."

"And when I learned that Violet had left me this property, I didn't know what to make of it. My knee-jerk reaction was to sell and get out. No point in being burdened down with property, right? That went against all my beliefs."

"Yep, that's you all right."

"But it wasn't because I needed the money out of the place. I could buy it or sell it or give it outright to you."

Daphne stared at him. Would he do that? But then would that mean he'd be leaving town too?

"But the more I stick around here—"

"Do you mean the more time you spend with a certain someone?"

"That's implicit. The more time I spend here, the more I can see undertaking something a little more permanent. Like knocking down walls, making Violet's duplex a single-family home."

"So, you could rent it out as an Airbnb?" She was joking but she hoped he didn't plan to do that. Obviously, that would be over her dead body anyhow. But that wasn't worth pointing out.

"So that maybe, eventually, if things go in the direction I'd like to think they're going, you and I could live there together."

Daphne's eyes grew large. "For real? You aren't just kidding with me? And we'd make a big kitchen—with a huge island—"

"Large enough so that I can dine on you, preferably."

A little jolt ran through her. "And can we keep the back deck just as it is?"

"I was thinking maybe fortifying the privacy screening on it a bit," he said. "Maybe figure out a way to make it soundproof while we're at it."

Daphne pointed upward. "You know that tricky Violet. She was always trying to matchmake me, and one was worse than the next. She sure did get the last laugh."

"Oh, I don't think she's laughing up there, I think she's grinning from ear to ear."

"Me too."

Thank you!

Thank you so much for reading **Hard to Get Over**! I hope you enjoyed it! If so, please help others find this book:

1. Help other people find this book by writing a review.

2. Sign up for my new releases email so you can find out about the next book as soon as it's available and get fun giveaways.
   http://eepurl.com/baaewn

3. Like my Facebook page.
   www.facebook.com/jennygardinerbooks

And I love to hear from readers! Let me know what you think about my books! You can write to me at jenny@jennygardiner.net, and visit me on the web at www.jennygardiner.net.

Read on for a teaser of the next book in the Hard to Get series – *Hard to Get By*!

About *Hard to Get By*:

Hard up…

Sunshine Ferguson had finally gotten her Zen on. After years of being an uptight staffer for a hotheaded senator, she'd been forced to switch careers, changed her name to something more cheerful and less evocative of the implosion from her last job, and became a yoga instructor. It was the furthest thing, career-wise, from what she'd been doing. She really needed to nourish her soul upon being fired when she got caught accidentally making out in a dark bar with a staffer of the candidate trying to take the senator's job. The loud-mouthed press secretary proved once again that men were never to be trusted, though at least his blabbering their secret finally forced her out of the job that had been toxic for a long time. Life was finally good for Sunny. She was calm. She was imperturbable.

Until the very man who blew up her career—and ultimately absconded with her job—shows up in her class, seeking to find his own nirvana.

Read on for a sneak peek.

Chapter One

Two Years Earlier

MEGHAN Ferguson had had it with work. As cool as the job sounded on paper, in reality, being a press secretary to a U.S. senator was all-consuming, and when it came time for re-election, it went from bad to worse. Only the dirty truth was, it was always re-election season. There wasn't a politician to be found in the Washington, D.C. area who wasn't campaigning for a job or appointment or another cushy six years with great government benefits and freebies out the wazoo twenty-four/seven. All they did was jockey for more, more, more. The DC gravy train kept them fat and happy. And it was lowly staffers like Meghan who suffered for it. Cause it meant that Meghan spent her waking hours churning out steaming heaps of bullshit trying to make her high-maintenance boss look good. And when they were legit in the battle for re-election, it was that much worse, because then she constantly had to deal with the bombardment of slurs hurled at her boss from his opponent—make that more often his opponent's press secretary—and it all just got quite exhausting. It used to be sort of exhilarating, but now it was just hellish, and a bit depressing.

She'd been working in publicity for the senator for the better part of the last decade, and she was spent. Today had been a long day. Her boss' challenger had held a press event earlier, in advance of a debate tomorrow night, at which he referred to the senator as a "dimwitted womanizing loser" or some such nonsense. The senator flipped his shit over that one (and while he wasn't necessarily dimwitted, or a loser, he was certainly a creeper of a womanizer). Worse still, the publicist even called out Meghan as an inept press secretary who spread lies and misinformation. Even she was seething by the time she'd turned off the presser, and was this close to marching to wherever it was their headquarters were and telling his newest press person (the candidate seemed to have trouble keeping one in his employ for long) to cut the crap. Because that person could control this behavior and was failing to do so.

Which was possibly why she found herself having one too many cocktails on her own at Bottoms Up, her favorite little local near her Capitol Hill rowhouse, and becoming engrossed in conversation with a handsome stranger who held tightly to every word she uttered. It was kind of nice for a guy to give her his undivided attention, even if whatever she was blathering on about was complete nonsense.

At the moment her witty repartee had to do with the desperate need for another baby panda at the National Zoo, because, well, it was a conversation about as far away from politics as possible, which was exactly what she needed. And a baby panda would be something she could obsess on rather than how much of a loathsome bully her boss was. Earlier in the day, before that debacle of a presser, the senator had reamed her for something he'd said that he decided to blame her for—because isn't that how it worked? Accountability was apparently for underlings. She was just over the whole damned thing.

She'd taken on this job with absolutely no political skills whatsoever. She'd been working for a local television station in a miniature media market and yearned to be in a city. So, she ditched her reporting aspirations and took a job for which she had no great qualifications, except for bullshitting quite successfully during her job interview.

"Maybe instead of breeding pandas, the National Zoo should breed something more exotic, like blue whales," the cute guy next to her said with a grin. He had gorgeous, straight, white teeth. That worked well with his thick, light brown hair and eyes that vacillated between green and golden. Or maybe that was her third mojito that was seeing that. Cause who had golden eyes but for lions. Or billy goats?

She swatted the cute guy on the shoulder. "That's impossible," she said. "Blue whales are, like, ginormous. They weigh over three hundred thousand pounds! What're they going to do—have a holding pen in the Potomac River? And where do you get the mate for the girl blue whale?" She leaned closer to his ear. "Not gonna lie: I'd pay good money to watch two blue whales go at it—it seems like an impossible task! Once we were at a bar in Ocean City and stood on the back deck overlooking the bay and watched thousands of horseshoe crabs mate. It might have been the alcohol that made it fascinating, but whatever, it kept me mesmerized. That sword thingy, gets in the way." She jutted her arm out from her nose, imitating it.

She started to laugh and tapped the bar so the bartender would fill her up asap.

Meghan tucked a few strands of blonde hair that had escaped from her tight bun behind her ears, then thought better of it and pulled the hair pins and elastic band out, freeing her long hair and giving her head a vigorous shake. She hadn't realized it was bringing on a headache until now.

The guy pulled out his phone. "We have to see how they do this."

Hard to Get By

Meghan saw him typing into his browser, "Blue Whale Sex."

She rolled her eyes. "Are we seriously going to watch blue whales fornicate now?"

"Hell, yeah!" He laughed, then began to read. "...they begin to form pairs, where a male will follow a female around for weeks on end...though sex is not a foregone conclusion."

Meghan wagged her finger. "Dude, let me tell you: my girl ain't putting out for just any old blue whale. Even if he does stalk her. She's gonna hold out for a well-endowed whale—"

"...sometimes a second male will approach the pair, at which point the trio will race along the surface of the water."

"I'm sorry, but you best not be suggesting a blue whale threesome. That would displace like half the water in the ocean." She took a swig of her drink. "Besides, my girl is not a promiscuous whale."

"Yeah, well, just like everything else in nature, the guys fight and whoever wins gets the girl."

"What female wants to end up with the pugnacious asshole, though?" She shook her head. "I mean really. What a stupid system." She rolled her eyes.

"Maybe it's more romantic than that," he said. "Maybe it's that these two strapping, male, uh, leviathans, want her so much they're willing to fight to the death for her. Or maybe one is defending her honor when the other one insults her."

"You mean like he called her fat?" She parroted her hands like a puppet talking. "'Hey tubby, you better lay off the krill, sweetheart.'" She growled. "Men are the same the world over."

Meghan had recently gotten out of a relationship with a guy she'd dated since college. He actually had told her one time she needed to lose a few pounds or he'd leave her. She should have left him then and there, but she dragged it out longer until she found out he had been two-timing her with a girl like three years younger than her from her sorority who'd recently moved to DC. Whatever. She didn't need that kind of toxic juju in her life. Maybe she needed to find herself a well-endowed blue whale instead.

The guy frowned. "I resemble that comment," he said. "Not all men are assholes."

She nodded, plucking a maraschino cherry from the nearby fruit station at the bar, and popped it into her mouth. "Okay fine. Not all of them. Only ninety -nine point nine nine nine percent of them."

She chewed on the cherry and swallowed it, then stuck the stem in her mouth, twisting it with her tongue and her teeth till she secured it in a knot, then pulled it out of her mouth. It looked like a tiny pretzel.

"Ta da!"

The cute guy's eyes opened wide. "Whoa! You did that? With your tongue?"

She laughed to herself. Likely his own tongue would be hanging out, drooling at the notion of someone with such lingual dexterity.

She waved her hand. "An old party trick. Used to keep the free drinks flowing at parties."

"Aren't drinks always free at parties?"

She shrugged. "Good point. Maybe that skill didn't help me as much as I thought it did." She grabbed another cherry and repeated the stunt. "Nevertheless, I figured it was a talent I could employ when desperation set in."

"And you're feeling desperate?"

She shook her head. "Nah, just, oh, I dunno, in the mood to tie a cherry stem with my tongue."

"Can you teach me how to do that?"

Hard to Get By

She pursed her lips. "Hmmm... you have to pinky swear if you succeed that you'll not share this with anyone. Only a select few can join the club."

He arched a brow. "Ahhh... it's like a secret society?"

She nodded, pulled another cherry as the bartender scowled at her, and popped the cherry in her mouth.

She gave a tug on the uncomfortable underwire of her bra, sat up straighter, then held up her pointer finger. "Okay, first off, you need to have a long stem."

"The bigger the better, then?"

Her mouth lifted at one end. "That goes without saying."

"Are we talking about the same thing here?"

"If you have to ask..."

He windshield-wipered his hands as if erasing the discussion. "Continue."

"Obviously you have to pop the cherry gingerly." She burst out laughing.

"I had no idea this was going to be such a sexual thing."

"Everything is sexual. Even blue whales. Well, maybe not baby pandas."

He shrugged.

"Now this is counterintuitive, but if it's stiff, you want to make it soft."

"Well, that is totally *not* sexual."

"Truth." She high-fived him. "Rarely is limp good. Okay, now's when your tongue gets busy." She could see his eyes growing wide. She was having fun fucking around with his head. She also kind of worried she'd grown too hardened and cynical with her job that she would talk this way to a complete stranger in a bar because she was so fried from work. But oh well... "Press the center of the stem to the roof of your mouth with your tongue, forcing the two ends toward your front teeth. You're going to clamp down on them as you sort of force them to criss-cross with your tongue, forming a little loop. Then you take one tip and coax it through the hole—"

"This is definitely no longer PG-rated conversation."

"We're talking about cocktail fruit."

"But are we, though?"

She squinted at him. "Honey, I don't even know you." She laughed. "Now push the stiff part of the stem into the hole, then press down with your teeth to secure it. *Et voila*, you have a tied stem that will make all of your friends green with envy." She quickly popped the straight stem into her mouth, tied it in a matter of seconds, and held it up for him to see.

The cute guy leaned forward, his lips inches from her ear. "In about three seconds flat I'm afraid my tongue is going to be green with envy that that inanimate cherry stem is having all the fun around here."

Ahhh… the moment of truth. Until Now, Meghan was having fun just yanking this guy around. But he was awfully cute. And had a fun sense of humor. And when he got up close to her like that, he smelled rather delicious—like a crazy good combination of sandalwood and the Mediterranean Sea and maybe a hint of bergamot and lime. Although that lime was likely just her mojito. Whatever. Maybe it would be fun just to see what he tasted like too. She grabbed one more cherry, popping it into his mouth. "Meet me at the end of that hall, just after the exit to go downstairs to the rest rooms." She tapped the tip of his nose with the cherry stem and hopped off the barstool.

Hard to Get By

Holy shit. Was she for real? Well, yes, she was for real in that she was unbelievably beautiful—that wavy, blonde hair, once she pulled it out of that tight bun, made Kirby McCaffrey want to fist his hands in it while doing unspeakable things with her. And those aquamarine eyes, so clear you could see down to her soul. Her body was nothing to scoff at either—granted she was sitting so he couldn't quite tell the whole effect, but she had a nice set of tits. And Kirby was decidedly a breast man, so that's all he needed to stir things up. But when she got up and walked away and he was able to take in the bigger picture, yowza. She was stunning, with that form-fitting wrap dress hugging her ass, and those sexy heels that weren't too high—but instead looked professional, which is the look he preferred. Not stripper heels, which left nothing to the imagination.

He couldn't believe the turn of fortune he was experiencing tonight. Never in history had such a cartoonishly unnatural piece of pseudo-fruit become such a turn-on. He almost felt like a pervert, like he just discovered he had a cocktail fruit fetish or something.

He looked at the bartender who tossed him another cherry. "Go get 'em, boss." The guy said with a grin. Was it that obvious? He had to wait a minute at least to tamp down the burgeoning hard-on that was making it hard to stand. But he couldn't risk her slipping out a fire exit, so he stood, took a deep breath and advanced the troops, as it were.

He wandered down the narrow, dark hallway, passing a few folks returning from the bathroom. He walked past the exit door and the passageway grew dimmer still. His eyes adjusted to the dark and he looked about ten feet away and she was standing there, waiting for him.

He approached her and removed the stem from the cherry, slipping the fruit between her lips as he took in the stem between his, manipulating it with the tip of his tongue with no success.

"Let me help," she said, leaning forward and slipping her tongue inside his mouth, coaxing the stem away with her tongue. Somehow as she stroked his tongue with her own, she managed to maneuver the stem into a knot, then passed it back to his mouth. "See. I told you my party trick could come in handy." She grinned.

He pulled her closer and angled his head as he pressed his lips to hers, savoring the tiny moan she let out as their tongues tangled, taking the place of that now-discarded cherry stem. Kirby ran his hands up and down the woman's back, trying to find purchase somewhere, anywhere. His mind was running crazy with longing and while he couldn't believe he was suddenly mashing faces with this strange, gorgeous woman in the grimy back of a bar, he wished he was doing it within footsteps of her bedroom.

She paused for a moment, breathing hard. "I don't even know your name," she said, her eyes looking momentarily startled. "Although maybe it's better that way."

Was she suggesting anonymous sex? Which sounded alluring, but he wanted to know more about this woman, not just have a wham-bam moment with her.

"I make it a point to not get past first base without knowing a woman's name," he said, reaching for her bottom and pulling her toward the telltale bulge in his pants.

"So, is this what this is, first base? Making out wildly in a dive bar in the dark?"

"Maybe the bases are loaded, and we're waiting for that swing and a hit to send that fly ball into the stands?"

She shook her head. "Sorry, no home run tonight. Not simply because I still don't know your name, but also because my boss has a big debate tomorrow. I've got to get some shut-eye cause tomorrow's going to be a long day."

She pulled back and extended her hand to shake his. "Name's Meghan, by the way."

He squinted. Fuck to the fuck. She was seriously about to walk away, leaving him with a bad case of blue balls for his troubles? Impossible.

"Meghan. I'm Kirby. Can I maybe get your number and we can get together some time?" Fact was he, too, had a crazy day tomorrow, as his new boss also had a debate. Only in a town like DC would you have a coincidence like that.

She waved her hand. "Thanks, but I'm really not interested in anything. I just got a little carried away. Must've been the maraschino cherries. Or the copulating blue whales. Whatever. Great meeting you, Kirby. Have a good life."

With that she turned and walked away, leaving Kirby to groan and curse his bad luck. Then again, this was his first day in Washington, and his boss scored big points at his presser today, and he got to make out with a hot woman for no apparent reason. No reason to not see this as a win.

Chapter Two

MEGHAN kept thinking about that Kirby guy the whole day long. Even while she nursed a mojito-induced hangover, still he was lurking in the recesses of her throbbing head. Speaking of throbbing, it was impossible not to notice the guy was packing an impressive appendage. Maybe she should've taken that thing out for a test run. Except that she didn't have time for boys and their toys right now. Work was all-consuming, and she and men didn't mix well. A fleeting handful of kisses in the dark with a stranger would have to do.

Her desk phone buzzed and she picked it up.

"The senator wants you down here now!" It was Theresa, his bitchy and demanding secretary, happy to yell into the phone and accelerate her pounding headache. God forbid she start out the call with something a bit more genteel. Like maybe "Hey, Meghan! How's it going? I'm sorry to bother you but just FYI the senator is being a raging asshole right now, and he's screaming for you, like, yesterday. Good luck and I'll keep you in my prayers!"

Instead, she just served as his surrogate of vitriol, paving yet one more layer nastiness Meghan had to navigate her way through.

She grabbed her iPad, her purse and her notes and raced down the steps and into the senator's private suite.

Hard to Get By

"Where the hell were you? I was yelling for you! Don't you come when you're called?" The Senator had a scowl on his face, as usual. His bad combover was dangling on his forehead, and he looked like Squiggy from that old show Laverne & Shirley.

She straightened her dress and combed her fingers through her hair. "Sorry, sir. I came as quickly as I could."

"Where are my talking points?" he stepped into his bathroom, not even shutting the door, and started to pee. What was proper protocol for when your boss didn't have the common courtesy to shut the door when taking a piss? And was she supposed to hand him the file folder with his talking points while he had his hand on his little wee wee, taking a wee wee? And how could she do that without looking at it. It was gross enough that he'd tried plenty of times to interest her in said wee wee. Blech. He was old and ugly. Nothing about that man's penis would ever come in contact with her. She'd opt for celibacy instead.

He reached his free hand behind him, demanding his papers. "Hurry up, I don't have time to waste."

Evidently not if he was still urinating. She wanted to see how he'd get the papers out of the folder one-handed.

Instead, he finished peeing and zipped up, not even bothering to flush or wash his hands as he grabbed the talking points. "Come on, you're making me late."

The debate was being held at a network studio about three blocks away. Normal people would walk, but instead his driver was at the ready to hasten them off.

They popped into the car, raced the three blocks to the studio, the driver opened the senator's door—so much for chivalry—leaving Meghan to scurry after him like an abused dog seeking the attention of her cruel owner. A handler named Janie from the studio greeted the senator and didn't even

Jenny Gardiner

bother with Meghan as she led them to an elevator. They took the elevator to the eighth floor and got out.

As they walked down the hallway toward the studio, Janie filled the senator in on timing. "Congressman Tanner is already in there with his aid waiting on you, sir," she said.

"Tell Tanner he can go fuck himself if he's going to play nasty," the senator said as I elbowed him in the ribs, reminding him that speaking to members of the media in that way was not conducive to the best coverage.

As they entered the studio, Deborah Mott, the anchor who would be moderating the debate stepped forward. "Senator DeLallo! So lovely to see you again!" she reached forward to shake his hand, the one he'd just used to pee with, but he pulled her in and kissed her on the cheek. Manhandling a woman against her will was a skill he'd mastered long ago. "Looking good, Debbie baby." He pinched her butt. Meghan wished she could fade into the darkness that enveloped the outer ring of the cold studio. Instead, Deborah escorted them toward the empty dais. DeLallo's challenger, Congressman Tanner, a boyish thirty-something military veteran with dimples and a golden boy smile, stood erect and waiting. Meghan wondered why she couldn't work for someone so easy on the eyes, rather than her boss, who looked much like those large rodents you see dragging a slice of pizza down the steps of the subway on YouTube.

"Senator, I'm sure you've met Congressman Tanner," Deborah said. "And this is his new press secretary, Kirby McCaffrey."

Meghan's ears perked up. Kirby. How many press secretaries named Kirby were in this town? She strained to look past her boss, past the anchor woman, past the congressman and there she saw him, in all his still-hot glory. Well fuck. Of all the guys she could have teased and made out with in this town, it had to be him?

"Meaghan?" he said a bit too loud. Meaghan pretended she was busy with papers she was perusing. "Meaghan? Is that you?"

"Who's Meaghan?" his boss asked him.

"Over there," he said, pointing straight at her. "That's the woman I told you I was making out with at the bar last night."

Jesus H. Christ on a popsicle stick. Really? Who tells their boss that sort of thing?

"Remember I told you about the gorgeous woman? But she wouldn't give me her number? But here she is—"

The rest of what he said faded away immediately, because the mercurial Senator Antonio DeLallo, the man whose capricious temper could swing wilder than a menopausal woman in a heat wave, turned to Meghan, flames practically licking from his beady black eyes. "You fucked Tanner's press guy? After what he said yesterday? Is there something wrong with you? You can't just keep your panties on, you just meet someone in a bar and the next thing you know you've got your hands down his pants?"

Count to ten, Meghan. Count to ten. She bit her lip and began to count: One. Two. Three. Four. Five. Six—

"You're fired and don't even bother returning to the office for your things."

"But senator, you don't know what you're talking about."

"I heard all I needed to hear," he said. "I'm not good enough for you but this little fairy boy is fine enough for you to have sex with?"

"I didn't have sex with anyone. Please." As much as she hated the guy, she needed the income. She needed the job. Her whole uptight identity was wrapped up in it.

"Out." His face had turned red and veins in his neck were bulging as he pointed at her. She'd witnessed this kind of rage in him before. It was almost a form of foreplay for him, when he wanted to impress women he was around he always screamed at staffers and intentionally humiliated them. He must've thought Deborah would find it a turn-on. Highly unlikely. He looked like a feral honey badger in heat.

But Meghan knew there was no placating him. When his fury became volcanic, the eruption would continue and there would be no reasoning with him. His poor driver would be stuck trying to talk him off the ledge. Either which way, Meghan knew she was officially jobless. Thanks to that loud-mouthed piece of shit guy she stupidly flirted with last night.

She turned to Kirby. "Admit it: I was right. All men are assholes. You included."

About Jenny

Jenny Gardiner is an award-winning #1 Kindle bestselling author who has published 37 novels, a memoir, and a collection of essays. Her work has been found in Ladies Home Journal, the Washington Post, Marie-Claire.com, Paste Magazine, and on National Public Radio. She is an occasional essayist on regional NPR affiliate WVTF-FM, and wrote a humorous column in Charlottesville's Daily Progress for over a decade as well as a food column for Cville Weekly Magazine. She has worked as a publicist for a United States senator, and as a freelance photographer, photographing such notable public figures as Prince Charles, Elizabeth Taylor, and the President of Uganda. She's been the volunteer coordinator for the Virginia Film Festival for ten years. She's really bad at math.

Find her at www.jennygardiner.net